"I KNOW IT CAN NEVER BE..."

His face looks so wise for his fifteen years. The sun has bleached his already blond hair and it tumbles to his forehead in a cascade of blond curls. His blue eyes appear bluer because of his deep tan, and his body is lean and hard. "I hope we can always be friends, Mike."

A strange feeling washes over me. I have a crazy urge to reach out and touch him. I feel the flush of what I'm thinking and it races to my face, making me look and feel like I have a terrific sunburn.

Todd laughs and throws back his head. "What's the matter, Mike? You're blushing."

"Hot flashes," I joke back with him.

"You and my mom," he says. "Seriously. Where do you think we'll be ten years from now?"

Independence Day

B. A. Ecker

INDEPENDENCE DAY is an original publication of Avon Books. This work has never before appeared in book form.

AVON BOOKS
A division of
The Hearst Corporation
959 Eighth Avenue
New York, New York 10019

Published by arrangement with the author
Library of Congress Catalog Card Number: 82-22810
ISBN: 0-380-82990-8

Library of Congress Cataloging in Publication Data

Ecker, B. A.
Independence day.

(Avon/Flare book)
Summary: High School student Michael comes to terms with the fact that he is gay, and on July 4th, Independence Day, decides to tell his best friend Todd of his true feelings toward him.
[1. Homosexuality—Fiction] I. Title.
PZ7.E1977In 1983 [Fic] 82-22810
ISBN 0-380-82990-8

First Flare Printing, April, 1983

Printed in the U. S. A.

WFH 10 9 8 7 6 5 4 3 2 1

TO MARK The melody of your spirit
sings through this whole book.
Thanks for being you.

Special thanks to Ray Palazzo of the Odyssey Disco in Asbury Park, New Jersey, to Jim Gammarano and Jim Ridsdale for their help in dealing with this sensitive subject.

CHAPTER ONE

"MIKE." I hear my father call me from downstairs and for one instant I think if I don't answer, he'll forget it. The second call is more insistent: "Michael."

I stick my head out the bedroom door. "What is it?"

"Turn that stereo off and go to sleep. You'll never get up in time for school tomorrow if you don't," he shouts back. I do as he says, then lie back on my bed with my hands under my head, staring at the ceiling. I seem to spend a lot of time these days in suspended states. Dad says it's because I'm sixteen. I wonder sometimes if he remembers how sixteen feels.

When I get depressed, I try to spend some time with my six-year-old brother, Jeffie. That kid is really a riot. Sometimes he spends hours spinning mindlessly on blue-sneakered feet, falling into a great heap, then laughing. I wish I could get back to that.

Jeffie is so normal. He laughs easily. When he's

angry he bursts into tears of outrage. He doesn't worry for one minute about what people will think. When he smiles, his grin shows great gaps where his second teeth have yet to sprout and his hair stands up in wispy little cowlicks all over his head. And he doesn't care. Isn't it wonderful to be six and not have to care?

Looking back, I know I was never like Jeffie. Or like my older brother, Steve.

I feel an aloneness, an isolation that I can't explain with words. Oh, on the surface I do all the right things. I have a girl friend named Trisha, I play soccer, I get good grades, I carry the groceries for my mother. But inside of me, I know I'm different. Sometimes the difference is vague and sometimes it is acute. When I'm alone in my room with the stereo playing, I try to learn about myself and what makes me tick. And sometimes after hours of thinking, all I have is more confusion.

You see, I have a secret. Something that all of my years of Sunday school have taught me is a sin. Is wrong. Sometimes I feel attracted to my best friend, Todd.

There. I said it. Sometimes saying it makes me feel better. I've never said it to anyone out loud. I've said it to myself in the mirror and I've said it in my thoughts a million times. But I have never had the courage to really say it.

There is a name for this thing I feel—a name with awful connotations. The rest of the guys on my soccer team spend a lot of time calling each other faggots and fairies. When they do, I cringe inside. Sometimes I join in the name-calling because I certainly don't want to be suspected. But inside it hurts.

I've gone to libraries to try to find out why I have these feelings that no one else seems to have. The books are endless pages of black and white. They say these feelings are caused by strong mothers and weak fathers. They say men with these feelings want to be women. I don't want to be a woman at all. What I assume from the books is that nobody really knows too much about the subject.

All I know is that the feelings I have for Todd are sometimes overpowering.

The library has one book called *The Front Runner* that deals with a young gay athlete. I really found some comfort reading that. But most books on the subject are as vague as the feelings I have.

Then, there's Trish. I love Trish, I really do. We've dated for the past two years and she loves me, too. We have a lot of fun together and when I'm with her, I feel good. But inside of me, in the secret place, my desires are for Todd.

Let me explain a little about Todd. Since first grade, we've been the best of friends. He doesn't have any idea about my feelings and I'm afraid if I tell him how I feel, he'll run away from me. So I don't say anything. If I can't be his lover, then I'll be the best friend he ever had.

We double-date a lot. Todd and his girl friend Marcy, and Trisha and me. The gang at school considers us a clique.

I'm getting drowsy. The last thoughts I have before I go to sleep are of Todd. The way he looks in his red-and-white football jersey, his blond hair blowing in the breeze as he runs...

"Mikey, get up." I struggle to wake up and stare into Jeffie's jelly-streaked face. "You'll be late for school," he says. "Come on, Mikey."

The sun is streaming through the windows of my bedroom, and my cat Grouch is sprawled out asleep on my dresser.

"Look at Grouch, Jeffie," I tell my little brother. He pulls a chair near the dresser and looks right into Grouch's face. "Hi, cat."

As I've said before, Jeffie is definitely neat. Grouch

extends a playful paw, and soon he and Jeffie are rolling around on the floor.

The phone rings. "Mike, it's Trish," Mom calls.

Trish wants to know if I'll stop by her house and walk her to school. She has a history project to carry and it's bulky—and what are men for anyway but to help damsels in distress? I agree to help her.

Mom hands me a glass of orange juice and offers to cook me breakfast. Some days she's so busy with her job as a real estate salesperson that I barely see her, but today she has the whole day off. Mom is happy working. I guess now that her family is launched and capable of looking after themselves, she can give all her energy to her job. Last year she was the top salesperson in her firm.

"Let me make you some pancakes, honey," she says. "I feel guilty because I haven't cooked breakfast in a while."

I smile at her and she tousles my hair and gives me a hug. "You're getting so grown up, Mike."

I hate to think how she'd react if she knew my secret. She would wonder where she'd gone wrong. I want to tell her that no matter what, nothing is her fault. She's always been there when I needed her, she's always been understanding. This thing is no one's fault.

I wonder if there are other guys at school with the same feelings I have. No one can discuss them, that's for sure. In health class they show us movies about sex. Sex is a man and a woman. There are no other options open to us. A man courts a woman, sleeps with a woman and impregnates her eventually. Then they all live happily ever after. My feelings are not even discussed as a possible way of life.

Once a girl in my health class asked about homosexuality. The teacher looked shocked. "That's abnormal," she said, looking over her glasses at the girl. "We won't discuss that here."

No one ever wants to talk about it. That's what makes it so hard. It's almost an invisible thing. Everyone knows it exists but no one wants to acknowledge it unless it's the guys in the schoolyard calling "faggot."

I finish my breakfast and walk Jeffie to school. He skips as we walk and hums a little tune. He has a baseball cap on his head at a funny angle and every few steps he bounces a little. It's almost as if a musician is playing a mystical tune in Jeffie's head that no one can hear but him. After he gets to school, I walk on alone to Trish's. She greets me at the door with a wide smile and a kiss. It's only lately that we kiss in public. Maybe it's because Trish is more liberated these days, or maybe it's because I'm into showing everyone that I'm just like they are.

She hands me a huge cardboard box. "I'm so glad you're walking with me. This thing is impossible. I hope Foxie is happy with it."

Foxie is the worst teacher at Randolph High. He always hands out assignments that are almost impossible to complete and he grades with this staggered grading system. When he gives an assignment he says that to get top grades you must do several things. He lists these on mimeographed paper, which most of the class ends up using as airplanes. Everyone hates Foxie. His attitude says, *I don't care what you kids want. I'm here to do what I feel is best and you'll have to accept that.*

Kids pick up on things like that. I'm sure most teachers feel kids don't think much about what's happening. But we do. I think we have every teacher pegged. The opposite of Foxie is this teacher named Greg Cranston. He's a math teacher and he really cares. One day when I was really down in the dumps, feeling overwhelmed with my problems, he came over and sat by me. He put his arm around my shoulder and said, "Mike, if you ever have problems you feel you can't talk about with anyone, come see me. I'm a good listener."

Sometimes I want to take him up on the offer, but I'm afraid to put my feelings into words. Except to myself. Safe in my own room.

After Trish and I have walked awhile, Todd joins us, and then, three blocks later, Marcy.

Todd looks great. He's wearing faded jeans and a new white shirt. He still has some of his summer tan left and his hair is sun-streaked. I always wanted to be blond. The blond look is always clean, always attractive. And Todd definitely has the blond look.

He teases me about carrying the oversized cardboard box. If girls want to be so liberated, he says, they should carry their own projects. In a way he's right. Trish spends half her time telling me that women should be equal to men, but as soon as something like this comes up, she cries, "But after all, I'm a girl."

Somehow, the two don't go hand in hand. It's not only Trish. Lots of girls are the same way.

When we get to school, we carry the project up to Foxie's classroom. He's seated at a desk in front, marking papers. He looks very old to me today. He looks up and barely acknowledges that we're there. Todd makes a mock bow as we leave the room. "Good day, Mr. Foxworth."

Foxie looks up over his glasses for an instant, then goes back to marking his papers.

"That guy's a real faggot," Todd says offhandedly and I feel a deep pain inside. But I smile like I'm supposed to.

Posters in the halls announce the upcoming Halloween Dance. Naturally the four of us will attend, but the thing that has me excited is that after the dance the entire soccer team is going to camp out up on Mount Laurel. It will be the last camping trip of the year and Todd will be coming along, too.

Two days of sitting around the campfire, singing songs and telling stories with no girls to interfere. Two days of being alone with Todd.

CHAPTER TWO

STEVE IS coming home from college. I think I admire Steve more than almost anyone else in the world. He's so smart. People always say that Steve got most of the brains in the family, I got the looks, and Jeffie got the personality. At least we all got something.

Steve is different. I'd say I'm in awe of him. Sometimes, when he's talking to Dad, I sit and listen and wonder if I'll ever be that smart. He's in college now, studying aeronautics. He wants to design the jet planes of the future.

Steve always liked planes. When we were small and shared a room, he had shelves full of model planes that he had carefully designed and painted.

Those models were Steve's pride and joy. He even had one hanging from the ceiling by a string, and when I was real young I used to imagine I could climb into it and it would carry me to faraway lands.

But one day, when Jeffie was about two, he got

into the room and destroyed all of the models. He was sitting on the floor with the small planes in splinters all around him and the paint smeared on his face, showing he'd sampled some of them. Steve was about sixteen then. When he saw the planes, he stood there with tears running down his face. He never uttered a sound but somehow it was worse than if he had screamed at Jeff. Jeffie didn't know. He was only a baby but even I wanted to smack out at him. Steve didn't. He just gathered up the pieces and threw them away. He never even yelled at Jeffie. But he never made another model after that.

Steve is very family oriented. I think when I finally get to college, I'll only come home for occasional weekends and on holidays. Steve comes home every chance he gets. Sometimes he brings his girl friend, Carole. They live together. I think it's great that he has someone to love and share things with. Carole is a great girl. She has bright blue eyes and freckles and she's a real tomboy. She can outrun both Steve and me in a footrace and she tells great stories. In many ways she's a lot more broad-minded than Steve, and he kiddingly calls her a "liberal." Dad says she isn't coming this weekend. Somehow, I sense that that means there's trouble.

When Steve gets home he comes up to our room and plops down on the bed. It's good to see him. After all, he and I have shared a room since I can remember. He used to sneak downstairs and get me cookies while I was still in the crib. And at night, if I was afraid, he'd pick me out of bed and take me in with him. One time I wet his bed and he didn't even get mad. "Accidents happen," he told me. Steve has this way of making me feel good about myself, but I know if he knew my secret he wouldn't be able to understand. Steve is a logical person and logically he wouldn't be able to make sense of this. I sometimes wish I could be like him and deal with things in that cool, calm way.

I feel sad because I have so much to share with Steve but can't. At least I don't feel I can or ever will.

Steve smiles at me and asks what's new in my life. I tell him about Trish and the upcoming camping trip and how the soccer team is doing. I ask how his life is going and see sadness in his eyes.

"Carole and I are having problems," he says. "I wish we could bring it all together, but we can't seem to. Sometimes life gets to be too much for both of us. All I know is how much I love and need her. Sometimes I think she doesn't need me nearly as much."

I want to comfort him, so I hug his shoulders. "I'm sorry," I say, because I can't think of anything else to say.

"I know you are," he says. "You love her almost as much as I do. Let me give you some good advice. If you love someone, hold fast to them. It's too easy these days to give up on relationships. Love isn't that easy to come by. So if you find it and you know it's right, never listen to anyone else. Just listen to your own heart."

I think of Todd and the way he tilts his head when he smiles and of how close we are. Would Steve be able to understand this kind of love? For one moment I want to tell him how I feel, but a sudden rush of fear stops me. What if he doesn't understand; what if it ruins our relationship? I don't think I could stand that. Steve is too important to me.

"Do you love Trish?" he asks.

"I think it's just puppy love. I don't love her with my soul the way you love Carole."

His eyes fill with tears that don't overflow. "I love Carole more than life. I only hope she learns to love me half as much."

He wipes his eyes with the back of his hand and

changes the topic. "How's school? How are you doing with Foxie?"

It's good to have this time alone with Steve. To sit and talk the way we did before he went away to college.

Sometimes he'd build us a tent out of an old army blanket and the two of us would crouch inside and talk about all kinds of things. Steve always made me feel secure. As if nothing could go wrong in my life as long as he was there. When I had nightmares, he would be the one to comfort me and chase away the devils that I was sure were hiding in the night. Once when I was eight and having a lot of nightmares about strange animals, Steve invented an animal trap to keep them at bay. To most people, it would have looked like a shoe box, but Steve had painted designs on its sides.

"I read all about this in a book," he said with all the wisdom of a twelve-year-old, "and these designs are guaranteed to keep you from harm." As long as I slept with Steve's shoe box nearby, I was never afraid again. If a dream should waken me, I'd hug the box close and go back to sleep, assured that no monsters could get me.

"Remember the shoe box and the night monsters?" I say to Steve.

He smiles. "I sure do. I read up in Dr. Spock's handbook about how to make kids not fear the night. It said to give them a security object, so I designed one for you. It sure did work, didn't it?" He smiles. "I finally got some sleep."

I love my brother. He is tall and lanky and his hair is short and curly. When he smiles his whole face lights up. There is no phoniness about Steve at all. I wish Carole could see all the good he has to offer.

"I think I'll call Carole," he says. "Do you want to say hello to her?"

I want to say more than hello. I want to tell her she is hurting Steve and to get to our house this minute to comfort him. But I don't. After he talks, he hands me the phone and I just make small talk. "Hi, Carole, this is Mike," I say. "Why don't you come home with Steve next time?"

Jeffie comes into the room and demands his right to talk to Carole. He stands and talks to her, twisting as he speaks. I think it's remarkable that Jeffie hardly stands still a minute during the day. Even in his sleep he twists and turns until his covers are all bunched up at one end of the bed.

But Jeffie has no nightmares and there are no night monsters lurking in his closets.

"When you come again will you bring me a surprise?" he says, turning on his best Jeffie brat-act. "How about some lollipops"—bargaining for all he's worth—"or some chocolate?"

Carole loves Jeffie and I'm sure she'll buy out the candy store before she comes again.

"I love you. Good-bye," Jeffie says easily and places the phone back in its cradle. He gives Steve his wise-old-man look. "I do love Carole," he says quietly. "She knows how to treat kids."

Then, suddenly he's gone. I think Jeffie should appear and disappear in little puffs of smoke. That would suit his personality.

"Hey, Mike, how about if we spend the evening together?" Steve asks me.

"Sure, let's," I say. "It's been a long time since we did anything together."

"Want to bring Trish?" he asks, and I guess I don't look too excited. "Want to ask Todd to come?"

I telephone Todd and he says he'd love to join us.

"Let's have dinner at a place near the ocean," Steve says. "At a nice place with some atmosphere."

"You mean instead of Burger King?" I tease. For years whenever Dad would ask us where we wanted to have dinner, we'd both say "Burger King." It's become a family joke.

"Hi, guys," Todd says as he arrives at the house a few minutes later. "This should be fun. Boys' night out."

As we get in the car, Steve answers him grimly, "The way my romantic life is going, it seems like the only option these days." Then he changes the subject: "How's school, Todd?"

"Ah, it's the same as usual. We all complain about too much homework. We both have Foxie and he makes life tough for us," Todd answers, encapsulating our school day.

"He was hard when I was in school, too, Todd," Steve agrees, "and usually the butt of a lot of our practical jokes. Once we put all of the erasers into the lights and he couldn't find them. But he never got the administration involved, he always handled it himself. Toward the end of my senior year I started to realize he wasn't so bad after all."

"He's a pain in the ass," Todd says bluntly, closing the subject.

We pull up to the Lobster Shack, overlooking the ocean. It's a beautiful night, and the ocean looks like a moonlit painting.

The waitress smiles at the three of us as we enter. "Want to see dinner menus?" she asks pleasantly. The restaurant looks like the inside of a ship, with tiny portholes on each side, instead of windows. The back of the restaurant is all windows and overlooks the surf.

"Can we drink here?" Steve asks the waitress, and she says it's all right. "I have some wine in the car," he says. "But for God's sake don't tell Dad I gave it to you."

We promise that we're both sworn to secrecy.

The wine makes us feel good—warm and open to good conversation. It's funny how sometimes a drink will ease tension and make everyone feel good. Too bad the feeling isn't real.

It's a great dinner. We laugh a lot and enjoy each other's company. "You guys never change," Steve tells us. "For so many years I looked on the two of you as the deadly duo. It seems the only difference is that you're both taller now."

After dinner we walk to the beach.

"Let's go for a swim," Todd suggests. "There won't be too many days left when we can swim."

The water is cool this time of year because it is already October and the Gulf Stream has shifted. The moon is lighting up the ocean and the sand feels cool on my feet. We go behind some rocks and peel off our clothes. Then we race to the water's edge and dive in, coming up laughing and gasping for air. The water is so cold it takes our breath away. We run and play, pushing and shoving each other, then falling into the foamy surf and surfacing again.

I watch Todd for a long time as he races with Steve at the edge of the water. His naked body is perfect and glistening in the moonlight. His hair is wet and pushed back from his face and as he runs his muscles ripple and tighten. How perfect he is. I have never felt this way looking at the nude body of a woman. I feel my face redden, although no one but me is aware of the way I am looking at Todd. What if Steve realized how I felt? Would he ever be able to understand? In the privacy of our room, he told me to hold tight to love, regardless of what anyone else thought. I wonder if he considered the kind of love I feel for Todd.

I want to be able to reach out and touch Todd. The wine is making me more daring than I would usually be. But my mind takes hold of the situation. Stop it, I tell myself. You'd lose Todd totally if he even suspected your feelings.

I pull on my clothes, much of the magic quietly

gone from the night. I wonder if I'll ever be whole and happy again? I sit and watch my brother and Todd running on the beach and jumping through the waves, totally unaware of my unhappiness. Later, Steve asks me why I quit so soon.

"I was really cold," I explain halfheartedly.

"Ah, Mike," he says, ruffling my hair, "you're just a sissy."

Why is it I take such offense at that word? I want to scream out that I'm not a sissy. I'm not different from either of them—I just have feelings I can't reconcile right now. Why does this attraction for Todd seem so natural to me when everyone and every book I read says it isn't natural at all?

I wish there was someone I could talk to. There will be no hand-painted shoe boxes to rescue me from the terrors of dealing with this situation. Nothing Steve can conjure up from Dr. Spock will take care of this one. I've got to think it out and really handle it on my own.

When we get home, Trisha calls. "Hi, Mike," she says. "I finally got my dress for the Halloween dance."

I try to act interested although I'm really not. "What color is it?"

"The most beautiful shade of blue," she says. "I want to give you a piece of the material so you can match my flowers to it."

Suddenly I feel annoyed. Of course I'll get her flowers. Why does she have to plan it for me?

As she talks, my mind drifts back to Todd and the way he looked running naked along the beach. That's far more real to me than dyed-to-match flowers for the Halloween dance. I wonder what Todd will wear that night...

"Are you listening to me, Mike?" Trisha's annoyed now. "You don't seem interested at all."

"I'm interested," I protest, lying through my teeth.

"It's just that Steve's home and I'm preoccupied with him. He and Carole are having problems."

"Steve should marry her," Trisha says flatly. That annoys me. She doesn't have any idea what she's talking about. "Girls like security," she continues. "I won't live with you before we get married."

"That's stupid," I say, not really caring whether she wants to live with me or not.

"Trish, I have to go. Mom's calling me because I haven't cleaned my room." I want to end this seemingly endless conversation.

She takes the hint and, sounding slightly miffed, hangs the phone up a little too hard.

"Are you guys serious?" Steve asks. He's overheard our conversation from his bed where he has his nose buried in a book. "It seems to me she likes you more than you like her."

"She can get to me," I admit. "For one thing she always worries about being like everyone else. I've begun to grow past that. But to Trish it's everything. She says you should have married Carole."

"Tell her to mind her own business. What Carole and I do or don't do is between us."

"Have you ever considered getting married?" I ask.

"Not yet," Steve says, "because if we did, we'd end up having a baby and what if it didn't work out? Things in today's world are shaky at best. I think everyone should try living together before they tie the knot."

"In some ways you're right," I agree, "but it seems like the older, more traditional marriages last longer."

"That's because people were different then. They just lived with their unhappiness. Nowadays people feel differently."

"Yes, but is it better?"

"We all want certain things," Steve says, "and for Carole and me at this minute marriage isn't right.

Getting back to Trish's wanting to be like the rest of the kids—that's the way people are. Kids especially. They act the same, they dress the same. They have the same haircuts and the same shoes. It's wanting to be a part of the group that makes teenagers do that. Even older people have a need to be accepted. We sacrifice a lot of ourselves to belong. Trisha is just like most other kids. By the time you get to college, things start to change. You start to respect people who are different, those who aren't a part of the mainstream. People who dare to be different are the leaders of the world."

I wonder if I will ever dare to be different?

Before we go to sleep, Steve goes downstairs and makes us both hot chocolate.

"I'm glad to be home this weekend," he says. "I needed to be near my family and I needed to talk. You're really important to me, Mike. I have high hopes for you."

Tears well up in my eyes—I'm touched by the way he feels about me. I turn my face into the pillow so he doesn't see the tears and he squeezes my shoulder before he turns out the light. "Thanks for listening," he says. "You help me to see things more clearly."

I realize he thinks of me the way I think of Jeffie. That thought is very unnerving to me.

CHAPTER THREE

MOM IS nagging me again and sometimes I think I can't take it. Dad is laid back and seldom says anything, but Mom is a nag. Her favorite topic this week is how much time I spend away from home doing things. Can't she realize I'm growing up and that my boundaries are getting wider?

"Mike"—Mom's voice is almost a whine, like Jeffie's when he wants his own way and isn't getting it—"I want you to clean your room before you do anything else today."

I try to smile, but realize even as I'm smiling that it's forced. "Can I do it later, Mom? It's our project day."

Project day is something the soccer team at Randolph High has always had. We get together once weekly to coach a team of small boys at the orphanage. And we've developed a real closeness with the kids who live there.

"Well, everything seems to come before your jobs at home," she says.

I'm tempted to say, "That's right," but I don't.

Finally she gives me an exasperated look and says, "Well, go ahead then."

The guys on the team love this project. It gives us a feeling of accomplishment—working with kids who need someone to care about them.

Todd is actually the most active of all the guys. He's formed this little-league type of soccer team with the smaller kids. For the past month he's been doing odd jobs to buy his team some athletic equipment. He bugged Coach Wheeler into giving him all of the older soccer balls and knee pads.

As Todd and I walk to the home, he talks about his project. "I almost have enough money to get all of the kids shorts and matching shirts, just like the other kids' soccer teams have," he says. "I can't wait to see their faces when we deliver the goods to them."

The kids greet him like he's a hero when we arrive at the home. They cluster around him and hang on to his legs, and one little boy pulls Todd's baseball hat off and wears it on his own head. Todd has such a wonderful way with the kids. It's as though he lets his whole macho guard down when he's with them. They wrestle and tumble around on the grass and then he suddenly turns into a coach. "Okay, men," he says to his team, "let's practice so we can hold our own in the matches that are coming up."

The men—most of them no taller than Jeffie—line the field and kick the soccer ball end to end. Todd cheers them on. When a child does well, he lifts him into the air and makes a big fuss over him.

One little boy gets hit in the face with the ball and a trickle of bright red blood starts from his nose. The child's face pales and he starts to cry. Todd swoops him into his arms and gently wipes the blood away.

Another little boy, hand on hips, almost too swaggering for a six-year-old, calls, "Faggot. Don't cry."

Todd takes on an air of authority. "Don't ever call anyone 'faggot,'" he says, confronting the small name caller, "because if you were hit in the nose, you'd cry, too. It hurts. When people are hurt, they cry. Don't judge, unless you want people to judge you."

"I'm tough." The little guy stands his ground. He has a light smattering of freckles and his blue eyes are a little defiant. "I wouldn't cry."

Todd lifts him into his arms, too. "You could cry. That's the point. It isn't bad to cry and show how you feel."

Tough guy, it's obvious, just needs some attention. Todd lifts him to his shoulders and walks to the edge of the field with both boys in tow.

"Here—help me fix Timmy's nose," he instructs the other child. He shows him how to apply pressure to make bleeding stop.

Todd really knows kids. The tough guy has suddenly taken control. His toughness has vanished as he carefully tends to Timmy. He pats Timmy's face with one grubby hand and wipes the tears away. "I know it hurts," he almost croons. "I'll help Todd fix you up."

My favorite is the youngest girl in the home. She has taken a shine to me and always has a stash of things she's made for me every weekend. She makes a presentation of her week every time I see her. "Come on, Mike, I wanna show you what I made."

"It's my birthday next week," she says, almost in a whisper. "I'm gonna be five."

"Gettin' old, Tina," I tease her. I like the way she makes me feel—needed. She pulls a parcel of drawings from under her bed. Yellow spots of color interact with reds and blues. At least she chooses happy colors.

"Beautiful, Tina," I say. "Can I take them?"

She grins and ducks her head, raising blue eyes to meet mine. "I made them for you, Mike."

After spending time with these kids, I have a glow that's hard to explain. Todd says he does, too. Most of the team see themselves as macho strong guys, but I see them at their very best when they're working with these kids. Each of us has learned so much from these children.

On the way home Todd and I stop off at the candy store for a soda. Todd has to treat me because Mom is withholding my allowance for real or imagined things that I owe her for—such as cleaning my room.

"Does your mother bug you?" I ask Todd and he laughs.

"My mom is great, usually, but she has this constant need to give advice. It seems to me her favorite word is *don't*. Sometimes I wonder if she was ever young herself. She says my hair is too long, my views are too liberal, and that I should have to work as hard as she did as a teenager. I'm sure my grandmother never told my mother *don't*. Granny's just not like that."

"Well, my mother is a royal pain lately. She fights with Dad about Steve and Carole and she always tells Dad it's his fault we're all so lazy. I love her but there are times I wish she'd just go away someplace for an extended vacation." I feel better after airing my feelings.

We finish our sodas and I go home to clean my room and try to keep the peace for now at least.

When I get home, I notice Mom has been crying. Her eyes are red-rimmed and glassy, and she's sniffling. As she folds the laundry, an occasional tear makes its way down her face and falls to the clothing. I immediately forget that for the past week she's been bugging me to death and hug her. "What's the matter, Mom?"

"Nothing," she says and keeps folding.

"Mom, what's wrong?"

"Dad and I just had a fight and I feel awful about it," she confides in one moment of weakness. "I want things to stay the way they were—with Steve and Jeffie and you being here and playing in the yard and needing me. But I have to realize that the three of you are growing up and that things will never be that way again. Because I still want to be an important part of your life, I express it in the worst possible way—I nag at you and Steve and that just makes all of us angry. Dad says I have to accept the fact that you and Steve are young men and that I'm still important but in a different way. I guess he's right."

She smiles at me through her tears. "Did you have a nice day?"

"Mom," I say in a burst of love and insight, "I still need you so much. But when you nag at me I react the way you would if I nagged at you. But because I'm angry doesn't mean I need you less or love you less. I just need some space right now. Can you understand that?"

We hug each other for a long time, then I smile at her. "And right now I'm gonna go up and clean my room."

Mom seems much happier. "Thanks Mike."

I survey my room. Mom is right: it is a disaster area. Clothes I've worn all week are flung in every corner, piled both on and under my bed. I take off a pillowcase and stuff the laundry inside. Then I collect the dirty glasses—there are nine of them in my room hidden in various spots—and carry them downstairs. I even dust and make both beds. It looks like a new room. Even Grouch is looking around like he's in a strange place.

I even decide to sort out my records. That is really a job. Most of them are in the wrong jackets, many aren't in jackets at all—so sometimes when I'm in the mood to listen to the Beatles, I get Barbra Streisand. I really have to get more organized in my personal life.

The record sorting takes more than an hour, then I start on my books. I make piles—one for books I've read a few times, one for books I haven't read, and one for books I own but never want to read. Then I decide I really don't want to give any of them away, so I put them back on the bookshelf. Books are like friends to me and sometimes reading and rereading them is like visiting a familiar place or person. I have some books I've read four or five times and each time I read them, I learn something new.

Steve always says I'm a junk collector; perhaps I am. But to me books hold value. So I carefully rearrange them.

"When you're an old man they'll find you dead in a pile of old junk," Steve once told me. "They'll have trouble removing the body because of the sea of litter and junk."

Maybe Steve's right. But you know something? I really don't care.

CHAPTER FOUR

JEFFIE IS going to be an elf in his school play. Funny—the part seems made for him. He spends every waking moment in front of my full-length mirror, rehearsing his lines. He puts on funny little faces and grimaces at himself. Sometimes he roars in his best monster voice but then he remembers he's supposed to be an elf and he cools it.

"Will you come to my play?" he asks me. "Will you bring Trisha?"

"I wouldn't miss it. After all, it isn't every day I get to be the brother of a star." Even Steve has made plans to come home for Jeffie's play.

I remember my first play. I was about ten and they cast me as a knight. It's funny, but the minute I put the costume on, I *was* a knight. I always admired knights. They seemed to be the epitome of manhood—so tall, so strong, so untouchable.

I had about ten lines in the play, which was about King Arthur. I really wanted to be the king but the stage director chose Roger Strawbridge for that part. Looking back, I suppose Roger was better suited for it. He was tall and strong and he had long pale hair that hung to his shoulders—very King Arthur, even in the fifth grade.

I guess it was about that time that I started to realize I was different from my playmates. Lots of them were into looking at their older brother's *Playboy* magazines. They never interested me. Oh, I pretended they were interesting, but somehow I always hoped I'd find one with pictures of nude men in it.

Even at that young age, I sensed that was wrong. I hid it and I joined in with Todd as he leafed through the girlie books. "This one is wonderful," Todd said once, looking at Miss December, wearing only a red Santa Claus hat. He made this big deal about hanging her picture in our clubhouse. That was cool until his mother found it. That was the end of Miss December and Todd was restricted to his room for three days.

Actually things were simpler then. The sexual things that I now view as secretive were allowed to be talked about. We would look at each other's body when we swam and make mental comparisons: Was I as big as Todd? Was he as tall as me? It wasn't dirty. It was just the way things were, back in those days. Now it's taken on a whole new meaning. And it has a different name.

The other night I thought about how much of my time is taken up in wondering who I am. I spoke to Steve about it briefly and he says it's normal for teenagers to become introspective. But I know it's more than just that. Todd is introspective. I'm hiding.

I'm listening to Jeffie's lines for the tenth time when the phone rings. It's Trisha and she wants me to go shopping with her. I consider it comic relief—getting away from Jeffie, who is sometimes very tiring, and going with Trisha, who can also be very tiring.

When I get to her house she gives me a kiss, even though her father is sitting in his television chair, looking at me with great suspicion, his gray eyes fierce-looking over his horn-rimmed glasses. I've never seen Trisha's dad with his glasses up on his nose where they belong. Somehow they always slip down, giving him an absentminded look.

"Hi, Michael," he says in an offhanded way. He's the only person I know who ever calls me Michael except my parents when they're mad at me.

"Hi, Mr. Lane," I answer because I don't want to offend him. I don't know what he thinks I'm doing, but he always looks at me in this suspicious way.

Then he always asks "How are things?" But he doesn't expect an answer because as soon as he says it, he gets engrossed in whatever is on television and forgets about me.

Grown-ups are a puzzle. I don't think I'll ever be able to figure them out. Maybe when I get older, the mystery will lessen.

I think one of my greatest fears is to end up like my father. He's a good man, decent and a hard worker, and he's always done everything he can for his family. But he has no life of his own. My mom says he always wanted to be a painter. But then Steve came along and there were more important things than dreams to be painted on canvas. Steve needed a home and food and a bottle of milk at night. Some of Dad's dreams died then. Then I was born and he put his paintbrushes away entirely. They're in the garage now, all covered with dust and buried behind lawnmowers and rakes. He never even looks at them. Once I asked him why.

"There are some things we have to give up as we grow, and the life of a painter wasn't realistic for me. I chose to have a wife and a family. The two don't mix."

But I could read the look in his eyes. If he had known how it would be, would he have given up everything? I can see how it could happen. But I won't let it happen to me.

As we shop, Trisha holds tight to my arm. When we see someone from school, she smiles and waves and holds on tighter. Sometimes I feel as if I'm strangling.

I guess I've always related to my dad. I consider that we are alike, both of us being creative, both of us being thinkers. Mom, Steve, and Jeffie are alike—they sparkle with lots of personality and they can talk to anyone. Dad and I are the different ones.

Sometimes I think I could talk to Dad about the feelings that are troubling me, but then I think again. Would it hurt him to know I am this way? Would he hate me, worse yet? I have no way to gauge his reactions, so I spend a lot of time sitting back and thinking.

I'm patient. I want to resolve all of those feelings today, but I'm realistic enough to know it will take a lot more time.

Trisha and I have lunch at the hangout. The booths are decorated in orange and black streamers, and a fat orange pumpkin grins at me from the counter. Everyone is talking about the dance. I can't seem to get into it and Trisha gives me a long, serious look. "Mike, what's the matter? You hardly seem like yourself. Sometimes these days I feel that I don't even know you."

I smile weakly and take Trish's hand. How can she know me when I don't even know myself?

Todd arrives and breaks up the serious moment. He slides into the booth next to Trisha and for a second I feel annoyed. Then I think rationally. Where else would he sit?

"Hey, Mike, can I borrow your extra sleeping bag for the camp-out?" he asks.

My mind is so full of thoughts that I have to stop and think about what Todd has asked. Oh, he means Steve's sleeping bag. I grin at him. "Sure you can—three dollars a night."

Everyone is excited about the trip. It's always fun to get away with just the guys.

"I hope Tom doesn't make that awful chili," Todd says, wrinkling his nose. Todd has always wrinkled his nose when he has feelings about something. He uses it as a sign of displeasure, a sign of being happy, a way of being sexy. It's one of Todd's secret weapons and he uses it well.

"You guys shouldn't even go." Trish pushes her hair back from her face. "How boring. To be stuck at Mount Laurel with no girls nearby. I feel sorry for you."

"Sometimes guys need a break." Todd says it before I have a chance to. "We'll struggle through it, knowing you girls are back here waiting for us."

The two of us walk Trisha home, then Todd and I go to my house. "I have a problem," Todd says. "Can we talk about it?" We go to the back porch where it's private and no one will be able to hear us. "I want to break up with Marcy. There's this new girl I met at the library this week and she has me crazy. But how will I ever be able to do it? The four of us have been together so long, it's almost family." He looks at me with his wonderful blue eyes, waiting for what I think is a good solution.

"I feel like such a heel," Todd goes on. "Marcy is always at home waiting for me to call. And here I am out having a great time."

"What's her name?" I ask, for the purpose of cataloging Todd's girls.

"Her name is Deidre." When he says her name his voice sounds like he's speaking of a goddess.

"Do I know her?" I ask.

"No. But, Mike, you'll love her. She's great. What a body, too." He shows me what he means with his hands. "I've been with Marcy so long that it's become a habit, but with Dee it's different. She's a real woman."

He pauses for a long moment and looks at me in his special way. "Have you ever desired anyone except Trish?"

I want to shout and pull him close to me and say, "Yes. I desire you." But I know I can never do that. So I pull the "younger days" act and say, "I'm always looking. A guy is dead if he doesn't look."

Todd smiles at me, a wonderful smile that lights up his face. He wrinkles his nose. "You son of a gun," he says. "You always seem so together, so cool. So you look too?"

That's right, Todd. I look.

My mom sees us on the porch and tells us she's just taken some cookies out of the oven. She's been baking cookies for Todd and me for years now. We go inside and Jeffie attacks Todd, hanging on to his legs.

"Hey, Todd, I'm gonna be an elf," he singsongs. "Wanna hear my lines?"

Todd and I sit in the living room laughing at Jeffie as he does his best to be the center of attention.

After the show Todd gathers Jeffie into his arms and holds him close. He showers him with loud kisses as Jeffie screams and struggles to get away. I watch the interplay and fantasize that it's Todd kissing me.

Later that evening I lay in my bed, half listening to the stereo, half thinking about the direction my life is taking. It's all so confusing. Nothing seems to be right.

To most people "gay" means a man with limp wrists and a lisp. I know I'm not like that. Perhaps this is just a stage that I'll outgrow tomorrow. Sometimes

I can almost make myself believe that's what's happening. But then I examine my inner feelings and I know the way I feel isn't a passing thing. It's too much a part of me.

I also feel like too much thinking is bad. The more I think, the less I seem to understand what's troubling me. It's as if I add more with each thought. What once seemed clear becomes unclear. I think I'm my own worst enemy.

I'm almost asleep, lulled by the music of the Beatles, when I hear Jeffie cry out. It's an urgent cry, not just one of his whiny cries, so I get up and go to him. He's sitting up in bed, his face flushed, his eyes large and glassy.

"There was a monster, I saw him," he cries, and when he sees me, he hugs me as if I can protect him from anything. I bundle him into my arms, blankets and all, and bring him to my room. When he finally calms down a little, I tell him about Steve and how he made me the magic shoe box. Jeffie listens to the story with wide blue eyes.

"Do you still have it?" he asks. "Or can you make me a new one?"

I nod and he hugs me closer, then falls asleep in my arms. Sometimes I love Jeffie more than anyone else in the world.

CHAPTER FIVE

EARLY ON the morning of the Halloween Dance, Dad asks me to take a ride into town with him. Usually he doesn't ask me to go along, so I hurry into my jacket and Nikes and hop into the car. It's almost like being a little boy again, able to spend time with Dad alone.

When Steve and I were small, Dad always saw to it that he spent some time alone with each of us. Some Saturdays he'd take us to work with him. It wasn't very exciting at the store, but we got to be alone with him and talk out things if we wanted to.

The store was big and smelled like tires. The floor was always polished to a luster and there were rows and rows of shiny bikes to be sold. Dad's secretary had a glass jar on her desk and it was filled with jelly candies. We were always allowed to choose a few from the jar. And we were allowed to sit at Dad's desk and play "boss."

Dad's office was comfortable. It was like him.

Bookcases lined one wall and they were filled with books on old art prints. It was as if this place away from home was an area where he could retain at least a little of his old life.

One Saturday he took me to a museum to see an art exhibit. "I thought you'd enjoy this more than Steve would," he told me. I remember being thrilled because to me it meant we were more alike than he and Steve. Perhaps we were.

Anyway, Dad smiles at me. "This is just like the old days," he teases me, "when we used to spend Saturdays like this."

I want to tell him how much those afternoons meant to me and Steve, but the words don't come. Instead I smile at him and say that I remember them too.

"Mike, I feel like something's troubling you," Dad says, "and I want you to know that when you want to talk about it, I'll be here to talk to. Is it girl trouble? Are you having a school problem? What is it?"

"I'm not troubled, Dad. I guess I'm just having growing pains."

Dad smiles at me and I know I have never seen a kinder face on anyone else. "I know I get preoccupied with work," he says, "but I want you to know that you, Steven, and Jeffie are the most important things in my life."

"Are you ever sorry that you gave up painting, Dad?" The question hangs in the air for a long moment.

"Sorry? Perhaps that's not the right word, Mike. Sometimes I wonder what might have been if I'd kept up with my art, but then I wouldn't have Mom and you three boys. Perhaps I'd be very lonely. There's something about having children that makes a man whole."

I feel a deep sense of loss for something I will probably never have. "But isn't it more important to be yourself? Don't you ever regret making the choice you did?"

He smiles, and love shines in his eyes. "Never for a minute, Mike. And that's an honest answer."

I always think of my father as a strong man. When I was smaller, he'd lift me up to his shoulders. I always felt so safe there. As if no one or nothing could ever hurt me as long as he was near.

I want to tell him. I want to blurt out how I feel and ask him how I can get over it and be like he and Steven are. But once again, the words don't come.

We go to the store and Dad does his business, then we go out to lunch. He lets me choose the restaurant and we have a nice meal. He says Steve will be home the next day and that he's bringing Carole because they've patched things up.

"How do you feel about Steve and Carole living together?" Dad asks me.

"I think it's okay. Everyone needs someone to love, don't they?"

"In the proper time," Dad says. "In some ways I think Steve's relationship with Carole may be a little premature. Some things have to wait until we're ready for them. If we rush them too fast, they don't work out the way they should."

Then he looks at me. "Do you think you and Trisha will live together when you go to college?"

"I don't think so, Dad, but that's a year away and a lot can happen in a year. But I think it's okay for two people to live together if they want to." I stand up for Steve in the only way that I can.

"I guess my generation gap is showing," Dad says. "When I was that age it was drummed into our heads that relationships had to do with responsibility. Today it doesn't seem as if that holds true. Kids live together and if it doesn't work, they say, then no one is the worse for it. There isn't any real commitment. I can't help wondering if that isn't wrong."

Dad sits back and smiles his quiet smile. He has no real idea of what's happening to me. I feel a sadness about not being able to tell him. What if he knew that my heart and soul were crying out for another man? Would that make him think less of me? Would he believe what everyone else in this world is saying about people who feel the way I do? Or would he still look at me with the same love and understanding that he has always shown? I want to tell you, Dad, I think, but I don't think I'm strong enough to take a chance on rejection. Not yet.

After lunch, Dad and I take a long quiet walk on the beach. It's a warm day and the gulls fly overhead. We don't say a single word, but afterward I feel better.

After we get home, I hurry to get ready for the dance. The dyed-to-match flowers are downstairs in the fridge; Mom has my suit pressed and ready to wear. Everything is the way it should be. Jeffie sits on the toilet as I shave and I put some shaving cream on his face. Just like Dad used to do to me.

Todd arrives before I'm ready and he joins the two of us in the bathroom. He teases me as I put shaving lotion on my face. "You smell pretty enough to kiss," he laughs at me.

I think, Go right ahead.

He takes the blade out of my razor and hands it to Jeffie. "Here, you shave now."

Jeffie does a perfect imitation of me, even to the point of making a face as he does under his nose. Then he douses his face with Eau Savage the same way that I did. He prances around the room in a feminine fashion. "Am I smelling good enough to kiss, too?" he asks in a high falsetto.

But when Todd playfully reaches out for him, Jeffie suddenly backs away. "Boys don't kiss boys," he says defiantly. "Boys kiss girls."

Todd just laughs at him. "He sure has it all together, doesn't he?" Todd thinks Jeffie is a riot.

We pick up the girls and as usual Trisha's father makes a ceremony about telling us to drive carefully. He looks at his watch and says we should be home by one. Todd, who is the world's biggest father-pleaser, gives him a speech: "We'll certainly respect your wishes, Mr. Lane. Mike and I will have the ladies home on time."

The dance is like every other dance before it. The music isn't good. The kids are all behaving differently than from what they really are; the girls are all caught up in a mute competition. *See who has the best flowers. See who has the most expensive dress.*

The punch is watery and the cookies are stale, and my math teacher Mrs. Cardell asks me to dance with her. As we dance I feel the stiff ribs of her corset and suddenly I want to laugh out loud. I feel I'm a player in a play, doing what he has to do, taking his cues and never muffing his lines.

After the dance we stop for a hamburger, and Todd and I talk about the trip the next day. The girls feel left out and Trisha gets pouty.

"I don't know why we can't come," she says to Todd.

"Because it's a guys-only weekend, that's why," Todd says.

We take the girls home first, then Todd and I have a chance to talk. He's spending the night at my house so we can get an early start in the morning.

"Steve and Carole will be here tomorrow," I say. "Too bad we won't get to see them."

Before we go to bed, we pack our knapsacks and get our sleeping bags ready. Then we lay in the beds and talk until late into the night.

"Don't you sometimes wonder what life is all about?" Todd asks.

I say I wonder about it a lot.

"How is Deidre?"

He laughs softly. "She's great. God, she makes me feel so good."

He says he has a picture of her in his wallet, so he gets up to get it for me to see. He is naked except for his tube socks, which have red stripes around the top of them. Carelessly he plops down on the bed next to me and I feel as if I cannot breathe. I want to touch Todd, and the feelings of wanting to do it are making me crazy.

He flips the wallet to her picture. "Tell me that's not the most perfect woman you've ever seen."

She has long blond hair and bright blue eyes that smile out from her photograph. I tell Todd that he's lucky. That she is a real catch.

He's pleased that I agree with him and he messes my hair. "You have to look for a new old lady, too," he jokes, "so we can be a foursome again."

He grows serious. "I'm gonna tell Marcy when we get back," he says. "I can't pretend anymore. Do you know how hard it is to pretend all the time?"

I look at Todd's face as he sits on the edge of my bed. Do I know how hard it is, Todd? I'm a master at pretense.

The next morning Dad wakes us up. Todd looks at his watch and says, "We've got exactly one hour, Mike."

We both shower, then gulp down a fast breakfast and we're off to meet the rest of the guys.

There are twenty-two of us going to the mountain in the rickety old school bus. We'll park at the base of the mountain and hike to midpoint for the first night. Then we'll hike to the top and come back down again. Coming down is so much easier than going up.

For the first few hours of the trip we go through all the male macho rituals. We call each other names, we talk about who's sleeping with whom, we compare notes. Then finally, we get comfortable enough to drop our covers and be ourselves. That's one reason I envy girls. It seems like they don't feel the need to always establish rules and pecking orders. Guys feel a need to do that. They really aren't as secure as girls are.

Our coach, Randy Wheeler, gives us all a big pep talk about how this trip will make us more independent, rugged individuals. "It's important for a man to be able to survive under any conditions," he says, and I almost laugh. Here we are with our expensive camping equipment, brand-new tents, and a whole slew of cooking utensils. "Under any conditions" makes it sound like we're going to war or something.

We play at being men during this trip. We brave blistered feet and bad food, but this certainly isn't a spiritual building experience. It's a camping trip. No more, no less.

The best part about it is being with Todd and having his undivided attention for most of the time.

It's hard to explain why I feel the way I do about Todd. He has a certain familiarity and a strength that I need. Todd can handle any situation that might arise. He has a calmness that I envy. He is also a very spiritual person and I doubt that he has ever done a mean thing to anyone. He always thinks about other people first. If someone needed something Todd had, he would hand it over without a second thought. Sometimes he's too selfless. He just reminds me of every good thing in this world. And more than anything I want to share my time with him.

That night, halfway up the mountain, we sit around the campfire and tell stories. Todd tells the series of Jeffie stories before I have a chance to. "Jeffie's the neatest kid," Todd says. "Today I was teasing him and he let me know in no uncertain terms that he wasn't a faggot."

It gets the correct amount of laughter from the circle.

"We all know you're a faggot, Todd," says one of the guys. "We know you wear lip gloss and curl your hair at night."

Todd's Jeffie story starts the whole gang talking and telling faggot jokes and stories. I cringe inside as they talk, but I remain silent. One guy tells how these two gays he knew wore dresses on the streets. "Everyone thought they were girls."

Randy Wheeler offers his two cents: "They are. Faggots think they're women."

Later that night I lie awake long after the campfire has died out. Next to me, Todd is sleeping, his breathing deep and even. I clench my fists and tears well up in my eyes.

"Don't believe them, Todd," I whisper. "None of it is true."

CHAPTER SIX

ON THE second morning of the camping trip, we encounter a mini-emergency. Randy Wheeler steps on a broken bottle and needs to have stitches. Somehow, being halfway up a mountain assumes dramatic proportions if someone is bleeding profusely. And Coach Wheeler is doing just that. He decides that Todd and I should be the ones to help him down the mountain.

Randy Wheeler is a stereotypical coach. He's lean and energetic with graying hair and a know-it-all attitude. But I'm glad for the chance to be able to help him.

First, Todd bandages the foot because he's had advanced first-aid training; then the two of us support him for the climb downhill. It's a tedious climb and finally near the bottom a ranger appears and sends for help. We spend the rest of the morning at the hospital and by now the glamour of helping has given way to boredom.

After Wheeler's foot is stitched, he limps out from the emergency room. He smiles broadly at Todd and I. "Thanks, guys. I know it was hard giving up part of the trip for something like this, but I really appreciate it."

Todd and I debate about going back up the mountain for the rest of the day, but decide we'd rather see Steve and Carole. "We won't let the girls know we're home," Todd says, and I'm glad. Those were my feelings, too.

Steve is surprised to see us and when he sees the blood on Todd's Levi's, he feigns alarm: "You guys becoming ax murderers or something?"

It's nice to see Carole. She has a way about her that makes me feel good. She hugs me close. "I'm so glad I got to see you, Mike," she says. I know she means it.

"Let's not waste the day," Steve says. "Let's take a hike ourselves."

We pack some sandwiches and sodas and decide to hike at Hampton Park.

Everyone in our town knows Hampton Park. In the center of it, surrounded by gnarled old trees, is a mansion where terrible things once happened.

The stories about the mansion grow as the years pass. It seems there was an old man who kept his daughter chained inside. She was a prisoner until she died. People say that late at night, if you listen carefully, you can hear her cries for help—even now. In fact, she was dead a year before anyone ever found her. There are many kinds of prisons—hers was physical, mine is in my mind.

I relate to that imprisoned girl. I wonder why she didn't plan and scheme to get free. Perhaps there was no way for her. All I know is that I always feel a chill when I walk into that house.

Carole hasn't heard the stories and she says she thinks the place is beautiful. Funny, I never looked at it that way. But for someone who isn't aware of the history, I suppose it is beautiful. Tall pines surround it and the wooden interior is hand-carved. It has a huge porch where children now run and play.

"It might be pretty now," Steve says, "but it once was a prison." He tells Carole the entire story with Todd and I adding anecdotes as we go.

Carole shivers though the day is warm for October. "That story gives me the chills," she says, and when she grabs my hand I notice her fingers are icy.

After we spend some time at the park, Steve and Carole decide to go off alone. "We'll see you guys later," Steve says, and they walk away hand in hand.

Todd has a bright idea: "I'd like you to meet Deidre! Are you up for that?"

I smile my best all-American-boy smile. "Sure, why not?" If Todd likes her so much, she must be a dynamite girl.

We take the bikes. Todd rides Steve's and I ride my own, and we pedal through most of the town.

"Where does she live?" I finally ask.

"In Marblewood, with her aunt and uncle."

Marblewood is the wealthiest section of town and I tease Todd about being after her money.

"Wait'll you meet her," he says. "You'll see that even if she was penniless, I'd be after her."

We arrive at a dark, older house and when we knock, a butler answers the door. It's all very impressive. It reminds me of an old Shirley Temple movie. I wonder if perhaps Deidre is also being held prisoner in a back room. But soon she appears and dispels this fear.

She is pretty, but more important, she has an air about her that attracts me. She smiles and gives me a kiss on the cheek. "So you're Mike," she says. "Todd talks about you all of the time."

"All bad," Todd notes, and Deidre laughs. When she laughs it sounds like the delicate crystal mobile in Mom's room being stirred by a breeze—all tinkly and pure.

"All good," she says, and her eyes grow serious for a moment. "So good that it makes me a little jealous to think of how close the two of you are."

She has hit too close to the truth for me to be able to smile through this. Todd saves the moment by hugging my shoulders. "We've been through so much all of these years," he says, "including carrying old Coach Wheeler down the mountain today to get stitches."

"Why?" she asks. "What happened?"

Todd's eyes get that little glow in them that means he's going to make up a story. He wrinkles his nose for effect, then begins. "You see, he spotted this lady fair at a campsite adjoining ours," he says, his voice taking on a secretive tone, "and he just had to be with her."

He smiles, then continues. "He didn't want us to know, so he waited until we were all asleep; then he crept through the night. We heard all this noise and assumed it was a bear or something. We started to throw empty bottles at him. One beaned him and as he fell he stepped on it." Todd's smile is smug. "End of story." He crosses his arms to signify the ending.

Dee doesn't know him as well as I do and she looks puzzled. "How did he know the woman wanted to talk to him?"

Todd and I laugh loudly. Then Dee laughs, too. "Todd, you're a liar."

"No, I'm a story teller, there's a difference."

I understand why Todd prefers Dee to Marcy. She wears cut-off jeans and her hair is tied up simply with a blue ribbon. She is like quicksilver and isn't so busy playing at being helpless.

Some people I like instantly and Deidre is one of them. I like her enough that I'm not upset at all the attention Todd is paying to her. Somehow she includes me in it. It isn't Todd and a girl and me—it's the three of us and I'm sure she's the one who has made it that way.

Her aunt and uncle aren't at home so the three of us sit at the biggest table I've ever seen and have hamburgers. Deidre cooks them and they are too well done, but I'm so hungry that I gulp them down.

"I hardly ever get to cook," she says.

Todd grins at her. "I can tell."

He always gets away with saying the worst things to people because he has this endearing, little-boy way about him. People never seem to take his teasing seriously. If I said the same thing, I'd probably get punched in the nose.

"Why don't you call Trisha and see if she wants to go out?" Todd says. "That way we can all go to a movie."

I don't want Trisha to intrude on the three of us and I can't understand why. But I do what Todd wants me to and call her.

"Is Marcy going?" she asks, so the job of explaining about Deidre falls to me.

"Nope," I say. "Todd's taking a new girl in town named Dee."

"Then I'm not going. It would be disloyal to Marcy." Trisha is hard to understand. I know she is Marcy's friend, but she isn't going with Todd, she's going with me. I guess I'm half relieved when she decides not to come.

We see a movie called *Divine Madness* with Bette Midler. I love it and so does Deidre. Todd says Midler looks like she belongs on Forty-second Street being a hooker. Sometimes I think Todd has some trouble seeing the beauty in people like her.

We both walk Deidre home and then we pedal the bikes back to my house. Todd and I say good night, then I climb the steps to my room.

Carole is sitting on my bed. Steve is nowhere to

be seen. "Hi, Mike," she says. "Steve and I just had a spat and he's gone for a walk."

"You guys are so close that there are bound to be some problems, especially with personalities. I know there are problems with Trisha and me, and we don't even live together." It sounds feasible to me.

"Our problems are more complicated, Mike," Carole says. I notice she has a hurt look in her eyes. "Some of the things are just too complicated to explain."

"Like how Steve talks a lot, but never about how he really feels deep down inside?"

"That's one thing," she says. "I feel like we don't communicate enough." I know this is one of Steve's problems. He can tell anyone how to solve anything, but don't get too close to how he feels about himself. I think of the day that Jeffie broke the planes. He must have been torn up inside but he never said a word. Sometimes silence is the hardest thing to deal with.

Carole pauses for what seems like forever, and when she speaks, her voice is so low that I have to strain to hear her. "Mike, I've met someone else." I think if she allows herself to talk any louder she will burst into tears.

"Why?" I ask. Then, "Who?"

"His name is John and for a long time we were just good friends, which is something Steve and I never were. Then it became more serious and I realized he had a lot to offer as a person. He fills the spaces that Steve doesn't. I've tried with Steve, I really have. But sometimes we have to have the good sense to know when to give up. I can't help feeling I owe Steve something—loyalty, devotion, something. We've been together for a year now. I think I've learned from the whole experience."

Suddenly two fat tears roll down her face. I feel totally helpless. I hug her and let her cry.

"Carole, do what your heart tells you is the right thing to do. That's the only way you can be assured that what you're doing is right. People have to listen to their hearts."

I hear my advice and wish that I could follow it. Do what your heart tells you. Oh, how I wish I could do that. It sounds so simple.

Steve arrives home and he comes into the room where Carole and I are talking. "Please excuse us, Mike," he says. "We have things to discuss privately."

At the same moment Mom yells up the stairs, "Mike, come down here, I want you to run to Seven-Eleven for me."

Before I go, I take an apple from the refrigerator and Dad smiles at me. "How was the trip?" he asks.

It's too hard to explain all that has happened today, so I just smile and say it was great. Dad gives me a hug. I can't explain why that makes my eyes fill with tears.

CHAPTER SEVEN

IT'S MONDAY NIGHT and things are quiet. Carole and Steve have gone back to college and I have the room to myself.

Foxie really loaded me down with homework, and for some reason I can't seem to be able to get into doing it. So instead I sit with my book propped open in front of me and my mind a million miles away.

Todd and I had an interesting conversation about Dee today. "I really love her," he said. "More than I've ever loved anyone. She's so special."

I feel a pang of jealousy. I know I have no rights in this area, but that doesn't change how I feel.

"Have you ever been in love, Mike?" he asks. "I mean really in love?" His eyes lock with mine and he waits for an answer.

"Sure I have. But not in the way you are," I answer.

He smiles at me. "It'll happen and when it does

you'll love the feeling. I hope you'll be able to talk to me about it."

He is still being my very best friend. I want to tell him, *Yes, I do know about love and the special way it makes you feel—I'm in love with you.* But I don't say anything. He gives me a puzzled look. "Mike, if you ever want to talk about anything, remember me. I'm always here."

In the past few weeks I've realized what I'm feeling has a proper name—homosexuality. I've tried to discuss it with many people. The first one was the school nurse.

"I'm doing a report for health," I tell her, "and I want to know some things."

She's always been easy to talk to. She's plump, and smiling, and she's been the nurse since I was seven years old.

"What do you want to know, Mike?" she asks, giving me a grin reserved for those kids she deems special.

"About sexuality," I say to her, and she blushes a little. "More especially, why some people are attracted to their own sex."

She gets a little irate. "That's sick, Mike. It's perverted. Those people need a doctor."

She grins again, but this time I realize it's an empty smile. "You shouldn't waste your time on that stuff, Mike."

Then I talked to Mr. Cranston. I'm getting to be an expert on laying out the subject to get the best feedback from people. Cranston was a mixture of positives and negatives. "I think any adult has the right to be what he wants to be," he says, "and I would defend the gays' rights to that. But personally I think they have some sort of emotional problem."

I wish I could find some neutral person to really talk to about these things. For now, all I can do is keep turning it over in my mind.

I'm still the same person as I was before. In the morning as I look in the mirror and blow dry my hair, I know it's me looking back. But inside I feel different.

If I had a choice in the matter, I would opt to be like everyone else. That would be so much easier. I think that's what everyone in the world wants. To be able to look at themselves and say, "I'm just like the guy next to me." People make a lot of noise about being different—about being individuals—but when it comes right down to the nitty gritty, everyone wants to be accepted. So I have decisions to make.

On one hand I have these desires, over which I have no control. To me, my feelings are as natural as breathing. I have definite romantic feelings for Todd. I want him to be with me and to share with me and kiss me. But I know it can never be, so my feelings are colored by a deep inner frustration. I worry about my parents. If they find out I have these feelings, will they look at me differently? Will they think I'm dirty or sick? Or will they be able to understand that love is never dirty?

I want people to like me. To respect me. If I let them know about my feelings, how many people will turn away from me? But on the other hand, if I don't let them know, how can I ever feel honest?

Sometimes I think it might be easier to pretend and end up marrying Trish. We could become the average married couple, having 2.5 kids and a dog and buying a cute little house in the suburbs. But inside of me, I'd rage with unfulfilled desires that Trisha could never satisfy. So would it be fair for me to marry her? Sometimes I think if I don't find the answers, I'll go crazy. And even as I try to analyze my feelings about Todd, they don't make sense or match up in any way.

I've always loved Todd, although in earlier years I didn't understand what I was feeling. Initially, I loved him as any child loves his best friend. But when did the feelings change? When did the simple love of a friend become something more? I've thought about that a lot and I think I have the moment pinpointed.

We are fifteen and we're walking along the beach. It's early in the fall, and Todd and I are talking about the summer just past and how it affected us.

"Let's sit in the sea grass and smoke a joint," Todd suggests. The two of us find the tallest sea grass and sit in the middle of it in the sand. The sun is still warm and it makes sparkles on the ocean. The sand feels silky and hot under my bare legs. Todd lights the joint and draws hard on it. We don't smoke a lot of pot, but this is one of those occasions when we do. "I wonder where our lives are going from here?" Todd says, suddenly introspective.

His face looks so wise for his fifteen years. The sun has bleached his already blond hair and it tumbles to his forehead in a cascade of blond curls. His blue eyes appear bluer because of his deep tan, and his body is lean and hard. "I hope we can always be friends, Mike."

A strange feeling washes over me. I have a crazy urge to reach out and touch him—to run my hands along his smooth body. I feel the flush of what I'm thinking and it races to my face, making me look and feel like I have a terrific sunburn.

Todd laughs and throws back his head. "What's the matter, Mike? You're blushing."

"Hot flashes," I joke back with him.

"You and my mom," he says. "Seriously. Where do you think we'll be ten years from now?"

I try to get a handle on what I'm feeling. Even as these feelings are surging through me, I know I'm not supposed to be feeling this way and I don't understand it. All I know is that the feelings are natural for me. Todd is talking about college but my mind isn't taking in what he's saying. I'm experiencing the start of a new way of life. I know for a fact that there has always been something missing in the way I feel about girls. I love them, I hold them, I like to kiss them. But what I feel this sunny afternoon with Todd is so much stronger.

The joint relaxes me and the flush leaves my face. It has been a moment of reckoning for me.

Suddenly Todd stands up and peels his shorts off. "There's no one on the beach," he says. "Let's go for a swim."

And as we'd done so many times in the past, we strip down and race for the foamy surf. But this time, it's different. The cold water washes over me and it feels good. For one second I can forget the feelings that are rushing in at me.

"We'll stay the best of friends forever," Todd calls to me through the roaring surf. I try to push away the feelings that are overwhelming me. But I can't.

In all of his innocence, Todd makes it worse. As we are walking back to where our shorts lie in a rumpled pile, he hugs me. His nude body feels warm against my own. The thin strip of white against his dark tan catches my eye, and the urge to hold him close to me and kiss him almost overcomes me.

"Mike, I love you," he says. "We've been so close, shared so much. We couldn't be closer if we were brothers."

I don't answer for fear that if I open my mouth, Todd will be able to hear the pounding of my heart.

Later that afternoon, I spent a lot of time in deep thought. I had so many new feelings to sift through. And for the last year, that's all I've been able to do—think. How did this happen to me? Why was I singled out? Why do I desire men when all of my friends desire women?

Did Mom give me different vitamins than she gave to Steve and Jeffie? Or is something inside of me twisted and wrong? Or, in the final analysis, are some people simply born this way?

I want to know all of the answers, more than anything else in the world. I need to have some peace of mind. Something inside me makes me feel less than other people. I wonder if it's because of all of the negative feelings people have about homosexuality?

Have you ever bitten into an apple that looked all red and shiny on the outside, but once you bit into it, it was bruised inside? That's how I feel. I can no longer look at myself as a whole person. Instead I see myself as someone who is hiding a dark, terrible secret that will ruin his life if it's exposed.

I want so much to be reassured that what I'm feeling isn't a sign that I've gone crazy—or that I am any less than what my brothers are. Sometimes I consider telling Mom and Dad. At least if I say it out loud, just once, to another person, I won't have to carry it myself. But I always reconsider, for I know once I say it, it's an issue that's there for all time. What if I start desiring girls three weeks from now? If I'd already made a statement, where would I be then?

In my deepest heart, I know I've always been different. But I don't want to be different. No one does, really. I have the same feelings about things as everyone else.

If I'm hurt I feel as bad as the next guy and if I'm happy the laughter is just as spontaneous as anyone else's. I love Grouch and make sure he has food and water. I listen to Jeffie's problems and try to help him grow up right. So, then, why am I so different?

From inside my head come the voices of my teammates: "Fag! Mike's a fag."

I feel shame. I don't know why. I want to tell them that names hurt as much as a physical blow. Perhaps they hurt more. I don't want these names hanging on me. I'm Mike. The same Mike that I was, the same Mike they know and respect. But if they knew my secret, I would never be the same Mike again.

I'm so engrossed in my thoughts that I don't hear Jeffie come into the room. He's dressed in a little green suit, looking for all the world like an escaped munchkin from the Land of Oz. He wears a green felt hat and his eyes glow brightly. "See my costume?" He turns around to give me the full effect. "How do I look? Terrific?"

Jeffie has all the self-image he needs. He's so positive about himself. I envy him for it.

I pull him up on the bed, glad for a chance to get away from my thoughts. "Tell me your lines one more time, wearing that elf suit," I say, and he's off and running. He even does a little dance with a mock bow at the end and both of us laugh so hard that the bed is shaking. From my bookcase, Grouch is regarding us with solemn green eyes. I guess he thinks we've gone crazy.

Mom comes up to see why we're laughing so hard. For her benefit, Jeffie does his lines again. She smiles at him. "You're quite an actor, Jeffie," she says. Then she gives me a long look. "Mike, if you get a chance it might be nice if you cleaned this room. The board of health might be in any minute to condemn it." Mom hugs Jeffie.

"Baby, you're a great little actor." It's been a long while since Mom has hugged me.

Jeffie draws himself up to his full height and pulls away from her. "I'm not a baby," he says indignantly.

Then she tells Jeff to get to bed and reminds me that I have to finish my homework. "That's more important than playing with Jeff right now," she says. "I'm going out to a meeting. You and Dad will have to manage things alone."

She closes my door and I hear her leave. Sometimes I wish I could talk to my mother, but I can't.

She just doesn't understand me at all. I tuck Jeffie into bed and toy with my homework. I can't concentrate, so I call Todd.

"Hi, Mike, what'cha doin'?"

"I can't seem to get into my homework. There's so much of it and it's boring. Damn Foxie and his ideas about education."

I hear a soft laugh from the other end of the phone. "Well, I don't care," Todd says. "Dee's here helping me." I hear him give her a kiss and I feel jealousy surge through me like an electric shock. "It makes it a lot easier when you have quality help."

There's a lump in my throat that is threatening to choke me. Todd is so happy. I wish I could be happy for him. But I wish it was me helping him with his homework and not Dee. That would make it easier. I feel as if someone has doused me with a pan of cold water. "See you later, Todd," I say.

"Okay, Mike. Dee says to tell you hi." He hangs up and returns to Dee and his homework. I get up and go downstairs where Dad is watching TV.

He looks up as I enter the room and smiles at me. "Hi, Mike. I hardly get to see you these days."

"What's on?" I ask and he hands me the *TV Guide*. "Pick something. It'll be nice to have company to watch with. Want me to make us a snack?"

My dad can't watch television without a snack, so I humor him and say "Sure."

I hear him puttering in the kitchen and soon he returns with two slices of cake and some chocolate milk. "See, I remember you always liked chocolate milk," he tells me. "When you were a little kid, a glass of chocolate milk would make your day. I used to give you chocolate milk when you were being crabby. It always worked."

My dad is such a dynamite guy. I wonder if perhaps I'm trying to replace him in my life, to assure myself he'll always be near even when I'm grown.

Todd is a lot like him, with a quiet self-assurance and a comforting way. I wonder if Dad was always so self-assured? I'd love to have known my father when he was sixteen.

"What were you like when you were my age?" I ask.

He rests his head on the back of the chair to think. He closes his eyes for a moment and I watch his expression. "I think it was the most painful time of my life," he says slowly.

In the background the TV is buzzing with a situation comedy where families never have problems that can't be solved, but my attention is riveted on Dad. "For me it was a time of great decision," he says. "I wondered who I was and how I fit into this world. I think we all go through that at sixteen. I was so idealistic. I thought everyone would always be the same. It's one of the realities that I've never been able to accept—the way we lose our idealism as we grow older."

"You haven't lost your idealism," I say.

He smiles at me. "That's because a part of me is still sixteen, Mike. I've never been willing to let it go."

"How old were you when you met Mom?" I ask.

"I met Mom when I was just seventeen, just when I thought there would never be a perfect woman for me." He laughs. "I'd been dating this big blond named Stella. I dated her because she had a loose reputation and at seventeen I felt I should have had some sexual experiences. But she intimidated me. I felt like an oddball. All of the other guys on the football team bragged about their conquests with the girls, but every time I tried something, the girls either said no or slapped my face. So I took on Stella. After all, the whole team said they'd slept with her at one time or another. But when I approached her, she started to cry. I felt like the world's biggest heel or the world's biggest failure. Here every guy on the team had scored with her, but when I asked, she cried. It took me years to figure out that the other guys had been lying."

I laugh at Dad's story because things really haven't changed that much today. The guys still brag, each one to match the stories of the others. I'd done it myself.

"I was starting to think perhaps there was something wrong with me and then I met your mother, and suddenly the world was a great place to be. She was everything I wanted and since that day she's made my world complete. Finding the right person to share your life with is important, Mike."

He gives me a word of advice: "Never settle for someone you aren't a hundred percent sure of, because if you do, the next day the right one may come along and it will be too late."

Dad continues, pleased with this topic. "At sixteen, I thought the world was ending if I had a pimple. I thought no one understood me. I felt like I was different from everyone else. I liked to paint, I also liked to play football. Somehow the two didn't go hand in hand in the fifties. Today painters can be any type of man, but back then, painters were supposed to be homosexual."

He said the word so easily. Did he see the panic cross my face? He smiled at me. He didn't notice. "My best friend was homosexual," he says, "but of course at sixteen, he wasn't sure what he was. Later in his life he sorted things out and now he has a different life-style of his own."

Dad has opened up the subject and I hunger for his views. "Was he a nice guy?"

"He was a wonderful guy," Dad says, "but the other kids made life hard for him. See, he didn't try to hide his differences. We talked about it a lot and we were very close. But he couldn't resolve his feelings. Once he told me he had always been in love with me. Of course, I never had any desires in that direction, but I told him I was honored that he cared so much about me. We still keep in touch. In fact, Jeffie is named after him. When Mom was pregnant, he called and told me since I was busy populating the world and since he wasn't, the least I could do was name the baby after him. So I did."

I am amazed. I know Jeff Hart. He's always been around. So big and strong and talented. "Jeff Hart?" I ask incredulously.

Dad nods. "Jeff Hart. But please don't judge him. I know how boys your age think. Jeff is a wonderful man."

Oh, Dad, I want to cry out. You've helped me so much without even knowing it. Suddenly I feel better about myself than I have in a year. I hug my dad and he pulls me close and kisses my cheek.

"I'm glad we talked, Mike."

"Me too, Dad," I say as I go upstairs to tackle that mountain of homework.

CHAPTER EIGHT

THE NIGHT of Jeffie's play is the first really cool night of the year. We're all going—Mom, Dad, Steve, Carole, Todd, and I. Trisha was going to come but she is in bed sick with the flu. So I sit in the third row of the school I attended for the first nine years of my school life and wait for the curtain to go up.

Jeffie is a nervous wreck and he shows it by becoming even more of a tornado. His felt hat is almost frayed from constant handling and he knows his lines without a hitch.

Sitting in the auditorium brings memories rushing back at me. Being in my first play and looking out into the audience for Mom and Dad is my clearest recollection. Once I spotted them, the rest was easy. But looking over all the faces until I found theirs was definitely traumatic. That's why I suggested the third row. Jeffie won't have to look so hard or so long.

Several of the teachers that Steve, Todd, and I had

over the years come over to talk to us. Jeffie's teacher tells Mom and Dad that he's the scene stealer of the show. That's easy to understand.

The lights go dim and the curtain goes up on a whole stage full of six-year-olds, all in different manner of attire. Then a small, bedraggled elf takes center stage. His small fists clench and unclench as he scans the audience in an almost frantic way. Only when the blue eyes light on our faces does he relax and start his speech. He plays to us: we are his audience. He delights everyone else in the process. I wonder if someday I'll be telling *Teen Magazine* that Jeff Ramsey is my brother. And that this is how he got started in show business.

"Isn't Jeffie great?" Todd says.

"He gets it from me," I agree.

Todd has always wanted a brother. Instead, he has a sister named Margaret Ann.

Margaret Ann is not the best person in the world to have for a sister. She is ten and she has freckles on her nose and braces on her teeth. She whines a lot and she tattles whenever she gets the chance. Her knees are knobby and her knee socks are always down around her ankles. I often look at her in total amazement. On one hand there's Todd, so handsome and wonderful. And then there's Margaret Ann. Oh well, maybe somehow the genes got messed up in the years between their births.

After the show, Carole gives Jeffie a package that's wrapped in red-and-white striped paper. He tears it open and finds a mini candy store—lollipops, candy bars, and gum. He hugs Carole tightly. "Thanks a lot. I know I can always count on you."

Todd and I take him to the hangout and let him have his pick of the menu. He orders a hamburger, a side order of fries, and two milkshakes, one chocolate and one strawberry.

Taking Jeffie someplace is better than taking a new puppy. He gets so much attention.

He begs for the evening to last a little longer and we agree to let him hang out with us for an extra hour. But before it's over he's slumped in the red booth with his elf hat smashed flat on his head and his box of candy clenched tightly to him. His eyelashes are so dark they look like smudges under his eyes. He looks small and innocent in his sleep.

Todd gathers him into his arms and we walk the four blocks to our house.

"Here's one exhausted elf," Todd tells Mom and he carries him upstairs to his room. He lays him on the bedspread among the teddy bears, the shoe box I designed for him, and several trucks.

Jeffie stirs and smiles up at us, the evidence of what he ate still smeared across his face. He reaches up both arms and hugs Todd with one, me with the other. "Thanks for letting me hang out," he mumbles before he falls asleep. I take off one small sneaker, Todd removes the other. Jeffie just turns onto his stomach and spends the rest of the night, I'm sure, dreaming about his stage debut.

Early the next morning I hear the phone ringing. It's the second call I've had.

"Mike," Mom calls up the stairs. "It's someone named Deidre." Todd's call was first. His grandmother took a turn for the worse and so his entire family drove to Connecticut to see her. Perhaps Dee thinks he's still here from last night.

I pick up the phone. "Hi, Dee."

"Just called to talk," she says, "because I spoke to Todd before he left this morning. We were supposed to go to a dance at my uncle's club tonight. Todd said he was sure you'd fill in as my date. How about it?"

I think of Trisha and wonder if it's worth the wrath

I'll have to face, but I don't want to let Todd down. "Sure, Dee. What time?"

I make plans to pick her up at 7:30 and then I dial Trisha's number. Her Mom says she's still sick, but she answers the phone anyway.

"Hi, Mike," she says. "Boy, do I feel awful."

I try to keep the relief out of my voice. "That's too bad, Trisha, I sure hope you're well enough to go to the movies tomorrow."

"You'll have to call me tomorrow. How was Jeffie's play?"

"He was a star," I say, unable to keep the pride out of my voice, "a real star."

"Well, he's a Ramsey isn't he?" she asks, as if that explains it.

Suddenly I feel like a rat. It isn't Trisha's fault that I have these feelings now. Yet sometimes I tend to put the blame on her. She bears the brunt of my frustrations. She really is a neat girl. "Call me later, Mike," she asks and I promise that I will.

"Feel better, honey."

Everyone else is still asleep, except Mom who has an early morning appointment. We sit at the table drinking coffee and talking.

"It's good to have some time alone with you, Mike," she says. "It seems our paths hardly ever cross anymore. You're so busy and so am I. It's good to have some time with you."

My mom can be a sweet person, too. She has a lot of creative energy and she is easy to talk to when she isn't nagging. I guess I'm a lucky guy to have such neat folks. While everyone else's parents are divorced and remarried, Mom and Dad are as much in love as they ever were. They still hold hands and sometimes Dad will suddenly kiss Mom right in the middle of a crowd. I think it's great.

I hope that someday I'll be able to have that type of relationship with someone. One of the biggest sadnesses I've faced is that my life-style will never allow me to have children of my own. That's the only part that hurts me inside. It isn't that I want to re-create myself, it's just that to me, children are the ultimate blending of two people who love each other.

But I think about Dad and how creative and talented he is and how he never gets to paint anymore. Perhaps my purpose is to do the creative things for him. Each of us is put here, I think, for some reason. Not everyone can paint, not everyone can be a writer. But each of us is unique in some way. And that includes me. I feel more positive about myself. It feels good.

"I'm taking Todd's girl friend to a dance tonight," I tell Mom and she smiles at me.

"You and Todd are almost like one person," she muses. "You have been so close for so long. I wonder how either of you will survive when you have to be separated?"

I wonder too, Mom, I think. I wonder if my heart will break and bleed and never be able to be put back together.

"Sometimes I look at you and Todd and I almost feel the bond between you. It's more than just friends," she says. "It's almost an energy." I wonder if somehow she knows, so I look at her with questions in my eyes.

"Since the two of you were just babies like Jeffie, there's been something special between you. When you were really small and sick in bed with a stomachache or cold, Todd would always call to see how you were. Once when you were in the hospital with appendicitis, we came home to find Todd asleep in your bed, holding your stuffed bear. His parents were frantic, looking all over for him, and the little devil snuck in here. Later, we asked him why and he started to cry. He said he was sure you were going to die because you were in the hospital. He thought that's where people went to die. Nothing would ease Todd's mind until we took him to the hospital to see you for himself. Then he was satisfied and even though he didn't get to talk to you, he felt better. You were sound asleep by the time we got there. He just sat in Daddy's arms and looked at you and touched your hair. Then he was content to go back home."

"I guess that's why I'm taking Dee to the dance," I say. "Because we're like one person in so many ways."

"What happened to Marcy?" Mom doesn't miss a trick.

"I guess you could say Dee happened to Marcy. She's a great girl," I add. "Perfect for Todd."

Some of what I feel about Dee is jealousy, but it's not because I don't think she's wonderful. I think anyone who spent a lot of time with Todd would make me have these feelings. But, first and foremost, I want him to be happy, even if I'm not included in that happiness. Marcy was never right for Todd. She could never live up to his sensitivity. They were more habit than relationship. Marcy, it appears, has gotten over her breakup with Todd pretty fast. The other day I saw her walking with a new guy and she looked just fine to me. So how upset could she be?

I spend the day doing chores around the house and at six I get ready for the dance. I shower and shave. I really don't want to shave yet, but I like the manly feeling I get from shaving. I always feel like a TV ad when I splash on the after-shave.

Jeffie takes up his seat on the toilet as I shave. "Got a hot date, Mike?" he asks and I give him a smile.

"Sure Jeffie, a real hot date."

"I thought Trisha was sick."

I make a silent gesture with my hand. "Don't tell anyone. It isn't Trisha."

"Oh God, Mike." Jeffie's face turns so pale that his freckles look like cinnamon specks on his nose. "Don't let her know. She'll have you killed." Jeffie is clearly a product of Saturday morning television.

"Don't worry Jeffie," I assure him. "She'll never know. It will be our secret."

"Oh God," he is still muttering as I leave the room. "Be careful, Mike."

I wonder if all six-year-olds think that jilted girl friends will kill you. Or is Jeffie just more in tune than most six-year-olds?

Dad lets me take the car and he doesn't even make an issue of telling me to drive carefully. That's a first.

I pull up to Marblewood and panic seizes me. I don't think I can remember which house it is. Then I see it on the right—the one with all the dark wood on the front.

I knock on the door and the same butler smiles at me. "Good evening, Mr. Michael." I feel like during the next moment, Bill Bojangles Robinson will tap-dance down the staircase, a curly-headed waif two steps behind him, but that's just imagination. Instead, Dee comes down the stairs, dressed in a beautiful white gown, her hair held back by a pink ribbon and flowers. She looks beautiful. Todd certainly knows what he's doing. If she wasn't Todd's girl, I might look twice at her myself. I stop mid-thought. Who am I kidding anyway? She is a beauty and I appreciate her for the goodness that is hers, but I'd much rather be spending the evening with Todd.

I have a box of flowers in my hand and she takes them and smiles at me. "You shouldn't have, Mike."

I say all the right things, then I meet her aunt and uncle. Everything is so formal. We drive to the club in a limousine with the butler at the wheel. I feel like I'm in a movie. This isn't the real world at all.

"It was so nice of you to fill in for Todd," she says. "You are a friend indeed."

"It's the least I can do for my best friend, and who am I to argue about taking the prettiest girl in town to a dance?"

She smiles at me and takes my hand. "If I wasn't in love with Todd, I'd certainly be in love with you," she says.

I want to tell her she made the right choice the first time. But I don't. Instead I say, "Well, if he gets to be too much for you..." and let the sentence trail off.

The dance is the same as all other dances, but this one is fancier. The ballroom at the club is decorated with orchids and bright streamers. It's all very proper and most of the men are wearing dinner jackets. I feel like my Yves St. Laurent sports jacket isn't fancy enough. I ought to be in tie and tails. We sit at tables lined with pastel-colored crepe paper and eat tiny sandwiches that are too small for my hands. We sip punch from elegant little glass cups and I almost feel like a giant in the land of the Lilliputians.

If ever I am rich, I refuse to get caught up in the life of the country club set. It's too hard, too stiff, too out-of-character for me. I like the real people—the ones who aren't so proper, who laugh loudly if they're amused, who cry if they're sad. I can't imagine any of these people crawling around on the floor with their kids the way my dad does with Jeffie. I know most of the children in Marblewood are raised by nannies, who tend to their manners and make sure they use the proper fork at the proper time.

"Are you enjoying this dance?" Dee asks and I say that I am, but she's a little too wise to believe me. "You don't like any of this, do you, Mike?"

I decide to be honest. "No, I don't. It actually seems too phony to me."

Dee giggles. "It is phony. But do you know what

I always do? I look at all of these people who are so pretentious and I imagine them sitting there in their nightgowns with curlers in their hair."

I look at these obese women with stiff curls pasted to their heads and imagine them in nightgowns. I have to laugh and Dee laughs with me.

"See, Mike? It works."

After the dance the butler drives us back to Marblewood and we walk to the porch and sit on the swing and talk for a few minutes. "Thanks again, Mike," she says.

I walk her to the door and she kisses me on the cheek. "I tried to imagine you in pajamas, Mike," she says, a sparkle in her eyes, "but I know you don't wear any."

With that, she opens the door and goes inside. My face is flushed. How did she know that, anyway?

CHAPTER NINE

SUNDAY DAWNS cloudy and cool. It's the kind of day that makes everyone shiver and brace themselves for what lies ahead—the winter. Todd calls me the first thing and asks how my date with Dee went. I'm still half asleep and my mouth feels like it's lined with cotton. But he wants all the details, so I force myself to wake up and talk to him.

"Look man, I'm calling long distance," he says.

"It was fun." I decide to tease him. "And by the way she said you don't have to bother to come back. She likes me better, anyway.

"I'm only kidding Todd," I finally say when I hear a long silence at the other end of the phone.

His voice is serious. "Don't kid about that, Mike," he says. "She's too important to me."

I tell him all of the details and add that he's lucky he missed it. Then I add, "How is Gran?"

Todd's voice breaks a little. "She isn't good at all,

Mike. I think she may die. I'll tell you about it when I get home."

Todd's Gran is really someone special. She's little and gray-haired and she's always been so spry. She hops around, reminding me of a sparrow. She used to make it to a lot of our little league baseball games and she always cheered the loudest for Todd and me. Life has to end at some point for everyone. But somehow no one is ever ready when it happens.

Todd and Gran always had a special relationship. I can still see them together if I close my eyes—Todd, small and wiry; his grandma following close behind him with a smile on her face.

Mom asks how Todd's grandma is and I tell her the bad news. Her eyes fill with tears.

"That's too bad," she says. "Todd loves her so much."

The news of Todd's grandmother upsets the day. Trisha calls before noon and invites me to her house for dinner. "I'm feeling a little better," she says, "but my parents want me to stay at home today."

I don't want to go and spend the day with her family, but I agree to it. I feel a little guilty about the night before and going will absolve me.

"How's Trisha?" Jeffie asks. He is staring into my face as I hang up the phone.

"She's fine."

He looks impatient. "Well, did she find out about your date?"

"No, she didn't, Jeffie, but if you keep talking about it, she will."

Steve and Carole come downstairs and they both look tense. "We're leaving early," Carole tells Mom. "I have a lot to do back at school."

Steve stands and shifts uncomfortably on his feet. He gives Mom a hug and shakes hands with Dad. Carole does the same thing but when she gets to Jeffie and I, she hugs us long and hard. "I'll be seeing you soon, Mike." She looks at my face as if she's trying to memorize my features to store away. "Thanks for being my friend." She turns to Jeffie and he leaps into her arms. "And as for you, little elf, you were adorable as always." A tear runs down her face and lands on Jeffie's hair. "I'll always love you, pumpkin, no matter what."

"I love you too," he chortles in his loudest Jeffie voice. "I'll always love you."

Although they don't say a word, I sense this is an ending. I hate it. They have always been a couple as far as I'm concerned. If I can't even deal with it, how will Steve?

About one o'clock I pedal my bike to Trisha's. I knock on the door and she opens it.

"Hi, Mike," she says, giving me a hug and kiss while her dad watches. "Let's go sit on the porch," she says and I follow her quietly.

"The years go so fast," she muses as she straightens the collar of my shirt. "Before we have a chance to think about it, the summer sneaks away and is gone."

"You sound like a philosopher," I tell her and she kisses me again.

"Do I?"

Lately whenever she touches me, I feel a surge of dishonesty go through my body. Even a month ago, I could lie to myself and make myself believe in what I was doing. The pretense gets harder and harder. Trisha senses it too, but she can't put it into words.

"Mike, what's the matter?"

"The matter? Nothing's the matter."

"Are you interested in someone else?"

Oh, Trisha, if only you knew, I think, but I shake my head. "Nope."

I long to be myself. To follow my feelings. To be able to say who I really am and what I'm all about. It's not in my makeup to be dishonest with anyone, most of all with myself. Where is all of this leading? What am I trying to prove by keeping it up? Trisha deserves better than what I can give her. I'm not honest with her—any more than I am honest with myself.

I look at her face and I want to cry. But I'm not sure if the tears are for her or for me.

"Remember the first time we did it?" she asks.

I blush. How could I forget? It was in the front seat of Todd's car during a party. Both of us were high and overcome with the idea of making love. The intent to actually do it wasn't there at first. We were just going to make out. It got out of hand and before either of us had a chance to think about it, we were having sex. It was fun, I have to admit that, but it wasn't as exciting as everyone kept saying it was. I worried that I'd hurt her and for days afterward it seemed she looked at me with scared eyes. I felt bad because I felt I'd been the instigator.

"I'm so glad you're the one that I first gave myself to," she says, "I really am, Mike."

I have to say something, so I say I'm glad too. "It was fun, wasn't it?" That seems like the right thing to say.

"I was so afraid I was pregnant," she confides with a giggle, "in my mind I started to think up names for our baby."

"Our baby" has an ominous ring to it. I gulp. "Good thing we didn't have to go through with that."

"What would you do if I got pregnant?" she asks.

Why do girls always want to know the answer to that? I'm sure I'd do whatever I had to do. "We'd get married I guess." There is a tightness in my throat. I don't want to get married at all.

Being with Trisha sometimes gives me the feeling of being bound and gagged.

The times after the first time were easier. Trisha

went to Planned Parenthood and got the pill, so there was no worry.

One night we had sex while we were baby-sitting Jeffie. We waited until he went to sleep; then we went into my room and Trisha sighed when I didn't hang up my clothes—just like Mom does.

"The board of health will condemn this room," she teased. If I'd have closed my eyes, I'm sure I would have seen Mom.

We were just in the middle of it when I heard Mom come in. "Mike, I'm home." Talk about panic setting in. I never got my clothes on so fast in my life. But then I decided it was better to pretend I was asleep, so Mom wouldn't get some clue from my openly guilty face. I think my parents have a sixth sense where this stuff is concerned.

I hid Trisha in the closet and hours later, when I was sure it was safe, I smuggled her out. Looking back on it, almost getting caught was as exciting as the act itself. And now I know why sex wasn't all it should be for me. I didn't want to sleep with Trisha—or any *other* girl. I want to sleep with Todd.

I've wondered a lot about what two men do together. I know I like the feeling of his lean, hard body next to my own. More than I like the softness of a girl. I want to find a book on gay sex. Sometimes I see them advertised "Shipped in plain brown wrapper," but what if Mom opened it first? How would I ever be able to explain that one? I can see it all now. I'd make some joke about it and she'd fling it in the trash and I'd never see it again. The library doesn't have this type of book on the shelves.

When I think of Todd and me, somehow I don't think about sex. I think of holding him and kissing him. I don't go any further than that in my fantasies.

"Let's go listen to some music, Mike," Trisha says. "You look a million miles away."

No Trisha, I think, just about two hundred miles away—with Todd, in Connecticut.

She lets me pick the records and I decide on classical. Trisha and I agree on music. We have the same likes and dislikes. We like the Beatles and some rock and most classical. We both hate country music with a passion.

Todd likes classical music, too. When we were younger we'd listen to classical music and put stories to music. Then we'd do shows, using the music as background. One time, we did a show about Adam and Eve. We were Cain and Abel. It was one summer when we'd gone to Bible school and were very impressed with the stories. So we dressed in tattered loincloths and used ketchup on the stick that Cain slew Abel with. And all without missing one beat of the *William Tell* Overture.

One time we dressed up in old clothes of Mom's. We were about ten and we thought we looked hysterical. Todd had on a floppy hat with a feather in it and I wore an old, flowered Easter bonnet. I liked the way the silky clothes felt and we both enjoyed smearing our faces with makeup.

Todd looked at me and I looked at him and we both started to laugh.

"Does this mean we're queers?" he asked me.

"What's 'queers'?"

"That's men who want to be ladies." He was wiser than I, at ten.

"Oh, I don't think so," I said. "We're just playing pretend."

"Good," he concluded. "I don't want to be like that."

And neither did I.

At dinner with Trisha's family, the talk centers around the changing state of the world.

"Teenagers today have no respect." Trisha's dad is looking over his glasses at me. "That's the biggest social problem."

"A lot of adults have no respect either. Where do you think teenagers learn it from?" I stand my ground, very proud of myself.

I'm surprised when he backs down. He sort of clears his throat with a fury. I've won one point.

After dinner, Trisha and I do the dishes and I tell her I have to get home because I have tons of homework.

"Mike, are you mad at me for something?" she asks. "When we're together I always feel like your mind is someplace else."

"No," I say, and I'm telling the truth, but she grabs my hand.

"I can't figure it out exactly, but you're different. We used to be so close. I always knew what was on your mind. Now I feel like there's a wall between us. I wish I was the girl in the *Fantastiks* and El Gallo would show up to tell me about who I love."

We both acted in the *Fantastiks* in freshman year. But then I was El Gallo... all wise, offering advice. Things have changed.

I wish I could blurt everything out to Trisha. But I don't; instead, I add to the pretense: "I love you, Trish." I kiss her. That's the easiest way to end the questions.

I go home and do homework until ten when a knock on the bedroom door brings me back to reality. It's Todd and his face is flushed.

"Come on in," I say. "What's the matter?"

He falls into my arms and cries rip from him in torrents. I hold him close while he sobs and cries until finally he can speak. "She's dead," he cries. "My grandma is dead."

I wish I could speak to him of heaven, of angels and God. But I can't. I love him too much to talk about things I don't understand. I do what I can by being there and letting him cry.

Finally his sorrow is spent and he lies on the pillow, lifting his tearstained face to me. "Oh, Mike, I'm not strong enough for this. I knew she was very sick and I wanted to be able to keep her alive. I never really thought she'd die. I love her so much."

His tears have now subsided to little silver streams that run from his eyes into his ears. I use my T-shirt to wipe them up as fast as I can. Todd gives me an intense look. "I'm so glad I can share this with you, Mike. No one else would understand the way you do."

We have been as one in many things. I could cry with him now, but I sense that I have to be strong.

"Love never dies, Todd, it's the one thing that lives on forever. Gran was a loving person. She gave you so much. And she gave you the ability to be able to share that love with other people. It will last your whole life and it will continue as those you love reach out and love others. It's a little like throwing a pebble into a river. A single splash makes thousands of tiny circles that encompass everything around them."

"It sounds good to me," Todd says and he leans up on his elbows. I notice his red Nikes are sandy and he gestures toward them.

"I ran on the beach for an hour before I came here," he says. "Somehow at the beach I feel her presence. She always loved the beach so much."

"Did you tell Dee?"

"No. Dee is the girl I happen to be in love with now," he says, "but you are so much more. We've always been together. Dee could be sorry and tell me everything will be okay in three weeks, but you understand. You are there. You loved Gran as much as I did, and she loved you, too."

We talk of the old days and we dig up stories about Gran and the role she played in our lives. At midnight, Todd stands to leave and I walk him to the door. He feels better. His face is blotchy, but at least the tears have stopped.

I open the door to let him out and he turns and pulls me to him. He hugs me for a long time and when he finally lets me go, he gives me a smile. "I'm glad you understand me," he says. "Who else possibly could?"

CHAPTER TEN

I AM uncomfortable in my navy blue suit. I've grown so much in the past year that the sleeves keep riding up and the pants feel too short. But it's the only suitable thing I have to wear to a funeral.

I hate funerals. I've only been to one before and I hated that too. A kid in our class died and we all had to go to the funeral. I kept thinking he was alive and they were burying him and how would he feel when he woke up under the earth.

Gran lies in a metal coffin, her makeup perfectly applied, not a hair out of place. But it isn't Gran. She always had her hair tied back with a piece of string from a bakery box, not a fancy satin ribbon. Her glasses are neatly folded into one corner of the coffin, as if she might reach out for them at any second so she could read the paper. I'm surprised there isn't one tucked neatly into the other corner.

Aside from family and friends, there are these efficient men in gray coats who seem to appear from nowhere to take care of things. "Oh, are you hot?" "Do you feel faint?" "Do you want some water?" I'd like to hit all of them. They are too professional and my grief is too private.

Todd spends most of the time sitting on the uncomfortable metal chairs with a blank look on his face. The person who is the quietest is Margaret Ann. She sits, a little wisp of a girl, with her knee socks around her ankles. She wrings her hands and doesn't speak. I take pity on her and take her outside with me.

"Want to go down the street for an ice cream cone?" I ask her.

She takes my hand quietly. "Yes. I'd like that."

We walk in silence and at the store we order two cones. She holds hers and gingerly takes little licks at it. It doesn't seem like her. She's too good. Too quiet. No whining.

We finish our cones and she neatly wipes her face and hands, being careful to throw the napkin in the trash barrel. Then we start to walk back. Suddenly in the middle of the walk, she flings herself into my arms and starts to sob. "Oh, Mike, my granny's dead."

I pick her up in my arms and let her cry as I walk along. Her arms are tight around my neck and suddenly she feels very much like Jeffie.

"Don't let Todd see me crying," she says. "Todd loved Granny most of all and if he sees me cry, he'll be more upset." So we sit on a bench. She sniffles and her face is a study of sadness.

She wipes her eyes with the back of her hand and that just makes her face look smeared. I take out my handkerchief and try to clean her face. Then I hold it to her freckled nose. "Here, blow."

She does and then she forces a little smile. "I'm sorry I cried, Mike." She puts a set to her scrawny little shoulders and she stands up and brushes off her dress. She takes my hand and we finish the long walk back. "Todd will never even know I cried," she says proudly.

Maybe I've misjudged this kid all along.

The ceremony is nice and then we drive about a hundred miles to a cemetery in Long Island. It's called "The Gate of Heaven" and it's very pretty. There's a lake and some ducks and beautiful flowers grow everywhere. "This is a nice place for Granny," Margaret says. "She always liked flowers and ducks."

Todd gives her pigtail a playful pull. "You loved her a lot, too, didn't you, baby?"

"Very much." Her eyes fill with tears that don't spill over. Todd hugs her close to him.

The funeral has been a growing experience for me. It's the first time anyone close to me has passed away, and I hope it's the last person for a long, long time. On the way home, we're more relaxed and Todd smiles a genuine smile for the first time in days.

"I'm glad it's over," he tells me when we get home. "She's at peace now. I'm sure of that."

He pauses a moment and looks deep into my eyes. "More than anything, I've come to realize how much you mean to me. I don't think I could have made it through all of this without you. Thanks so much, Mike, for caring and for being there when I needed you."

Oh, Todd, I think to myself, if you knew how much I care you might be surprised. Sometimes I want to tell him. I sense he would try to understand, and with his understanding perhaps I could deal with it better myself.

After we get home, I fall into bed and sleep soundly until the next morning.

That day, quite by accident, I hear some news that interests me. The guys on the team are telling stories about their weekends—who they got into bed and how much they drank. Then Tommy says he went into a gay bar by accident.

"I didn't know there was such a thing around here," he says, "but there is. You know that quiet little bar off of Water Street? That's a gay bar."

"Did anyone try to pick you up?" Coach Wheeler asks.

I feel like saying that even the girls don't like Tommy—why would anyone else? But I keep quiet—I'm interested in seeing this bar for myself.

"There were some guys dancing together," Tommy oes on, "and I even saw two of them kissing."

"Kissing?" Todd says. "You're kidding aren't you?"

"Nope." Tommy looks like a sage. "They were kissing on the mouth."

Some of the guys make gagging sounds and an uneasy laughter ripples through the room. But Todd isn't reacting in a negative fashion. Instead, he sits back on the bench and says, "I wonder what happens to someone to make them like their own sex. It's interesting. I don't think they can help it."

Coach Wheeler looks at Todd in amazement. "You want them guys chasing after you?"

"No, I don't want them chasing after me. But I do believe everyone has to be free to choose their own life-style—gays as well as straights."

If I wasn't afraid of the reaction, I would kiss Todd. And right on the mouth, too.

While we're having this whole discussion, Mr. Cranston comes into the room. He sits back and listens to us before he makes any comments. Then he speaks quietly. "It's a terrible thing for people to judge other people. No one really has that right, does he? Think about your own life. Aren't there some things you'd like to change if you could? Gays can't help being gay. I went through college with the nicest gay guy you'd ever want to meet. He was one of the most popular guys on campus, so full of love and talent. Two years after we graduated, he killed himself. He couldn't stand the pressures that society put on him every single day of his life—for something he couldn't help. Any more than Tommy can help having straight hair or Todd having blue eyes. If you want to single out people to pick on, look at people who hurt others. They're the ones to be teased and made fun of."

Coach Wheeler gives me a wise look. "He likes fags." Some of the team laugh, but it's a nervous laugh. The guys aren't stupid. They're all capable of reason.

Todd gives Coach Wheeler a long stare. "I happen to think Mr. Cranston's right."

"Think what you want, Todd" is his parting shot, "but let one of them approach you. Then we'll hear a different story."

I, meanwhile, am starting to make some real plans to get to this bar and see for myself what goes on there. Perhaps I'm not really gay after all. I don't want to seduce every guy I see. In fact, I don't want to seduce any of them.

I know that being gay is going to make changes in my life. Perhaps it will be more difficult, but I don't really have any other choice.

There are a lot of things that make up a total person. But I've noticed that if someone happens to be gay, that's all that's mentioned. It's the part that people notice first and last. It makes everyone around you judgmental.

I think, more than anything, that gay people have to be able to share their feelings just like straight people do. Such a large part of me feels chained up and wants to be free. I wish I could explain it to everyone, could make them realize that it's natural for me. I wish I could tell Todd. Would he turn away from me if he knew? Would he stop being my best friend? When we showered together in gym, would he always be looking at me to see if I was looking at him? Would he ever trust me fully again? But worst of all—and this is the bottom line for me—would he be able to see me as a whole person, not as someone who is flawed?

When I get home from school, Mom sends me for groceries and I ride past the bar. It looks the same as any other bar in town. How do gay people know that this is the place to go? For one minute I consider stopping the car and taking a look inside, but I'm not sure I look old enough. Some day I'll do it, when I work up the courage.

After dinner Steve calls and tells Mom that Carole has moved out.

"I knew they were having problems," I hear Mom tell Dad. "But that's almost all they can expect. Relationships take work. Today's young people don't seem willing to put enough effort into it. I wonder if living together without marriage is really an answer. Girls today don't seem to respect themselves enough."

"Don't you think you're being a little hard on Carole?" Dad says. "After all, so many young people live together today."

"All I know is that in my time, it wasn't done and the marriages lasted longer. Today as many people are getting divorced as are getting married, even with all this living together."

"Don't you put some of the blame on Steve?" Dad's voice is rising, something he rarely does.

"No. It's a man's world—it is now and always has been. Carole was the one who had to be strong. Not Steve.

"It was probably for the best. I'll never be able to understand her."

Sometimes I think Mom is all wet.

"She probably would have found someone else sooner or later anyway. It's a good thing they didn't have kids."

I can tell by Dad's silence that he doesn't agree at all. He doesn't like to fight, so he just shuts up.

Steve's heart is broken and Mom is saying it's for the best. I'll never be able to understand her.

When Dad tells Jeffie of the breakup, he bursts into tears. "I wanted her for my sister, she promised me," he whines.

"Perhaps Trisha will be your sister." Dad is trying to make him feel better.

"Oh no, not Trisha. She never even gave me a lollipop in my whole life."

"Jeff, you sound like all that Carole meant to you was lollipops." Dad sounds stern. "Surely that's not all you'll miss."

Jeffie sniffles for a few more minutes and then he digs his sneakers into the shag rug. "I'll miss her stories and her perfume and her kisses," he says with a wisdom far beyond his six years, "but if I think about that too much, I'll really cry."

CHAPTER ELEVEN

IN EARLY November we get good news—our soccer team is up for the shore regional championship. If we win that, then it's on to the states. Our school has always had superior soccer teams and this year is no exception. Steve played football. But I like to think that soccer takes more skill and endurance. Soccer players have to use their heads more—football is a game of brawn.

Todd and I celebrate the news by drinking a six-pack under the boardwalk. Coach Wheeler would have a fit if he knew we did that. He's so against alcohol or pot. At least once every three games, he gives us a lecture on the evils of alcohol and drugs.

Our last three games have been fought hard. We won them all by a score of 3–1, which is practically unheard of around here.

This year the football team isn't doing so well, so soccer has become the big thing. The halls are filled with posters about the soccer team. It's the first time that we're more important than they are around school.

We spend endless hours working out before the all-important conference game. Practices are filmed and then we watch them to see where we're making mistakes. At night I'm so tired that I don't even have time to think about my problem. That's probably good. I'm sure I need a rest from it. I'm even too tired to think about Todd much. With the championships and Foxie piling on the homework, I'm lucky I can think at all.

Mom's been good about letting me use the car to get to practices and Dad is bursting with pride. Jeffie is ecstatic. He plays soccer on the peewee team and he's a great little goalie in the making.

The day of the game dawns sunny and cold. Everyone is in high spirits and we sing on the bus on the way to the game. We're so sure we'll return home as winners. The coaches have scouted the team we're playing and they say we're superior. I hope we are.

About five minutes into the game we realize this team we're playing is every bit as good as we are. By the end of the first quarter, my hair is slicked to my head with sweat and Todd is breathless. The score is 1–1. Neither team is giving an inch.

Wheeler regards us with solemn eyes. "Let's get out there and win this one, fellas."

I look at him and suddenly realize what a total jerk he is. What the hell does he think we're trying to do?

But he manages to stir up something in the rest of the guys. After the second quarter we're winning 2–1. Our goalie is doing a terrific job.

There are a few tense moments but in the end we win 4–1. That means we get to go on to the states. The coach tries to hug all of us at once and we hug each other. We can hardly hold back our joy.

After we get home, the coach says we'll have to

come to his house to celebrate. That's too bad. Todd and I had our celebration planned. Todd has a bottle of Southern Comfort that he found at Gran's after the funeral and we were going to crack that open and get blasted.

When Todd picks me up for the party, he smiles and opens the glove compartment. "After the cookies-and-milk party, we'll celebrate a little more," he says. "I'm sure that's what Gran would have wanted."

The funny part is that he's right.

The party is fun. The coach gives each of us a little plaque with a special message on it and I'm sure that it will be one of those things that I move from place to place until I'm thirty-five and then debate its worth and throw it out.

The guys are all excited about the prospect of going to the states. We pledge ourselves to two more weeks of grueling practice before the actual matches.

After we leave Coach Wheeler's, Todd and I drive along the shore road, and although the night air is nippy we go up to the boardwalk. Todd pulls out the bottle and makes a ceremony of opening it. He gulps a mouthful and, from the face he makes, I'm sure the taste is overwhelming.

He holds it out to me and I follow his lead. After the first few mouthfuls, it doesn't taste as bad and before we realize it both of us are staggering drunk.

Todd's eyes are glassy in the moonlight and he slurs his words. "We won, old buddy, we won."

I sway as much as the ocean waves and agree with him. "We sure did, pal, now let's get on to the states!"

Todd grows serious and his eyes fill with tears. "Mike," he says, sounding a little like Jeffie, "Gran won't be here to see me win." Two tears make a shiny stream down his face.

He falls into my arms and although I am very drunk, I am aware of the feel of him against me.

He cries for a few minutes, then he laughs. "It's

really fate, isn't it?" he says philosophically. "Why couldn't we have won last year while she was still alive?"

His words are so slurred together that I can't really make them out. He breaks away from me and runs down to the edge of the water. He throws off his parka and starts unbuttoning his shirt. I try to stop him but he flings them into the water. The waves slap cold and foamy around our feet and I pull him back to the beach. He unzips his Levi's and then he's totally nude in the ice-cold night.

"Todd, are you crazy?" I yell and try to grab him, but now there's nothing to hold on to but his glistening wet skin.

He runs along the shore for a few more minutes, then collapses in the crashing surf. By now I am soaked and freezing and I pull him to his feet. I hold him in my arms and let him cry. The whole world seems fuzzy and hazy as we stand and embrace. I start to lead him back to the car, but suddenly I stop. I've dreamed about it for a year, but right now the courage to do it comes to me: the kiss is salty, a mixture of seawater and tears. We hold tight to each other, because if either of us lets go we will surely fall into the water.

I don't know how I get home. The whole time frame is lopsided now. I only know that when I wake up in the morning, I feel a deep sense of foreboding. How could I have kissed him? What will he say to me today?

At eleven o'clock he calls me. "God, Mike, I'm sorry, I really must have tied one on last night," he says. "Where are my clothes?"

I now believe there is a God. He doesn't remember.

"Well, you were busy throwing them into the ocean," I tell him.

He groans. "If I ever take another drink, kick me, okay?"

We speak of the upcoming game. Todd tells me he has an afternoon date with Dee. He also says he has an old box of toys for Jeffie and he'll drop them off on his way to the date.

"I'm finally giving up my Tonkas," he says, which makes me laugh. He always had more Tonkas than any other kid in town.

"What made you decide to give them up?"

"Well, I need the room for all of the trophies we're gonna be getting."

We'll be getting a big trophy for winning the regionals, but the state trophies are even bigger. All the guys on the team have their sights set on them.

"I'm going to get Dee a small replica of mine," Todd says. "Do you want to order one for Trish?"

"Sure." My heart isn't in it, but I know it will make her happy.

And it makes Todd happy. "She'll love it." His voice deepens. "She may even reward you." We talk for another half hour before Todd says he has to go.

Then he drops the bomb: "I had the weirdest dream last night," he says with half a question in his voice. "I'll tell you about it, if you promise you won't laugh."

He gets my promise then continues. "I dreamed you kissed me. Isn't that weird? I wonder if I'm going gay?"

My heart's in my throat. I think *I wish you were* but I know he isn't. He thought it was a dream—I guess I lucked out this time. I have to be very careful never to let that happen again. It's playing too close to home.

"Isn't that weird?" Todd is waiting for an answer.

"Yes, as a matter of fact it is weird. I wouldn't kiss you anyway. I only like brunettes."

We both laugh and it eases an anxious moment for me.

"Coach Wheeler wasn't in my dream either," he says, "and considering the subject matter, that's a wonder. Sometimes I wonder about him. I once read that the people who make the most noise over something like this are usually hiding something."

"I read that, too."

"Maybe our dear coach is a closet case," Todd says.

It feels good to be able to joke about the subject for a change. "Maybe he wears dresses when he's home."

"Where in the hell would he find heels to fit those big dogs of his?" Todd is laughing so hard.

It's a funny image: Coach Wheeler in a dress and high heels, still wearing his blue-and-white coach's cap.

The next few weeks are spent in a flurry of practices. Once again I hardly have time to think. That's good for me.

All of the problems fall into the back of my mind and I don't even have time to worry about Steve. Sometimes I hear Mom and Dad speaking of him, always with quiet voices. I want to ask what's happening but maybe I'm better off not knowing.

Calls to Steve are frequent and Mom now writes to him, too. But he doesn't come home as often as he did.

On the weekend of the states, he arrives home with two suitcases. "I'm dropping out," he says flatly. "I can't take the pressure." He opens the suitcases and starts to unpack.

"I guess I'm not that strong," he says simply. "I can't deal with Carole's not loving me. That makes everything in my life seem impossible."

"Did you try to work it out?" I ask.

He looks at me with eyes that seem years older than when I last saw him. "I've tried everything, Mike, except killing myself."

"No woman is worth that. Not even Carole."

"I'll never trust another one," he says. "I couldn't go through this hurt again."

"Oh, Steve, like you told me, love isn't easy. It's something you have to work at. Isn't that true?" I try to sound like the older brother.

"Sure it's true, but when you give all you have to give and it still isn't enough, you come away bitter," he says, sounding very old and jaded. Somehow he isn't the Steve I've always known and loved. This stranger sitting on the bed is too composed, too stiff.

"Maybe if you went out with other girls—"

"There won't be anyone else for a while yet—not until I can stop hurting a little."

Then he smiles at me. "How about the states? I can't wait to see them."

It's his way of ending the conversation. We won't speak of Carole again.

Steve asks Dad for a job, so he can at least work and earn his own way, and Dad, realizing that this is what Steve has to do at this moment, agrees that he can work for him.

The whole family comes to the game, even though it's quite cold outside. We look crisp and clean in our neat blue-and-white uniforms, but our bare legs have goose bumps on them. Until the game starts. Then we get sweated up in no time.

Once again, we all want to win. We want it so bad that the taste of the win is strong in our souls. At the end of the first quarter we are losing badly, 4–1. At the half it's worse. We don't seem to be playing as a team. Each of us is playing as a separate person. That's a killer for any team.

Coach Wheeler gets us into a huddle. "You're a bunch of glory boys!" he yells. "You've got to work together. It's as if you're all superstars instead of a team. Now get out and play together like a team. I know you can do it!"

His pep talk doesn't work this time and when the dust clears we have been beaten 7–1. I feel like crying. We wanted to win so bad. The other team is joyous. They shout and celebrate and hug each other, while we walk from the field with our heads down, feeling kicked and mistreated.

The ride back to school seems longer than it did when we came. No one says a word. The coach looks pissed off.

Is winning all there is? What happened to the old fun of playing just for the sport of it? I guess winning is important. At least by the look of my teammates and myself it is.

Back at the school Trisha and my parents are waiting for me. Dad is smiling as he hugs me. "Nice try, Mike."

Jeffie looks downright mad. He gives me a halfhearted grin. "It woulda been better if you won," he says. That comment gets him at least three pokes in his back.

Steve hugs me too and says, "You weren't bad, Mike, and there's always next year."

I can't remember when I ever felt so bad about losing. Trisha says we're invited to a party that would have been a celebration had we won. Halfheartedly I agree to go to it. It's better than sitting home alone.

Todd brings Dee to the party and although it starts out like a funeral, it gains momentum. Trisha spends most of the night ignoring Todd and Dee, and I have to run interference.

Then Dee drops her bombshell: "Trisha, it was nice of you to lend me Mike for the night. I really appreciate it."

Trisha grows crimson under her makeup, and I wonder if Jeffie is right. Perhaps I should run for cover rather than risk being murdered.

The explanation takes the rest of the evening. Right up until the time I'm walking her home, she's still asking questions: "Did you kiss her good night? Tell me the truth, Mike, I won't be mad." Trisha should work for Central Intelligence.

No, you'll just kill me, I think to myself, and what's more fun than getting killed?

Finally she makes her statement. "It's okay this time"—her eyes grow narrow—"but if it ever happens again, you're dead."

CHAPTER TWELVE

TWO WEEKS before Christmas, Todd and I go to New York for a long weekend. Todd has to look into some schools for art courses he wants to take over the summer and we both want to Christmas shop. I secretly have another reason. I've heard so much about Greenwich Village that I want to see it for myself. In some books it's called the gay capital of the world. I want to see what it's like. We stay at a hotel called the Shelbourne on Lexington Avenue, because it's in midtown and a central location.

The first afternoon, Todd has plans to look at a school, so I hail a cab and with as much confidence as I can muster, I tell the driver "The Village, please."

He leans back and says, "Where in the Village?"

"Oh, anyplace."

He guns the motor and we're off. We weave in and out of traffic in a way that defies description. When we get to a red light, he turns to me and gives me a know-it-all look as he chews his tobacco in a steady rhythm. Can he tell by looking at me that I'm gay?

Suddenly he brakes to a halt. "Here ya are, kid." He looks at me once again. "Better be careful. This place is loaded with fags."

"I'll be careful," I say, not wanting anyone to suspect I'm one of "them." I tip him fifty cents even though I think he's incredibly stupid.

I stand transfixed. The commotion and noise of midafternoon New York is overwhelming to someone like me who's used to the small towns of New Jersey.

I'm seized with a feeling that's a cross between panic and bliss. What if someone sees me here and tells my mother? I get hold of my runaway imagination and realize that no one here knows my mother or even cares.

Looking at the street signs, I recognize some of the names.

There are many men walking these streets holding hands. No one is looking at them. They share secrets and laughter together and it makes me feel good to watch them. I have the feeling of being home in this place. This is where I want to live; where I'll be judged on other things besides my sexual preference.

There is a small ice cream shop and I go inside to get a cone. The man behind the counter smiles at me, then asks my name. For an instant I think of giving him a fake name. But then I realize how foolish that is. After all, this isn't a movie.

I smile back at him and say, "Mike Ramsey."

"Are you new around here?"

"Yes," I say. "I'm just visiting."

"Where will you be later?"

"My friend is here with me," I explain. "If he decides to go home early, I guess I'll do some sightseeing." I am suddenly brazen: "Where will you be?"

"Around the corner at the piano bar," he says. "It's

number 212. Everyone goes there after work."

I'm walking out of the store when he calls, "By the way, my name is Jan."

I feel as if I'm in a dream. Why is everything so right here and so wrong just fifty miles away?

Several young men stop to talk with me. I want to ask a million questions, but I don't. Instead I just watch and listen. There seems to be some kind of unspoken language here that says, "Welcome. You are one of us."

One young guy in a sheepskin coat tells me it isn't that safe in the Village. "I know it looks like gays have full freedom here," he says, "but that isn't the case. There are people who drive through here just to yell 'faggot' from their cars, and there are gangs who wander the streets, looking for gays to beat up."

"Were you ever beaten up?" I ask him. He looks so serious and troubled.

"No, but one time some of my friends were walking down the street and a bunch of young straight guys attacked them. The gay guys were really beaten up—the straights had bottles and bats. One of my friends needed an operation because his arm was broken in three places."

"Didn't anyone help them?"

He shakes his head ever so slightly. "I saw it happening, but even I couldn't help."

"Why?" I am appalled to think he didn't at least try to help. His eyes grow dark.

"Because then they would have beaten me up."

I sober instantly. Even here, in the middle of their own territory, so to speak, gays have to contend with ridicule and beatings. Why can't people just leave us alone?

Afternoon fades into evening and Christmas lights decorate the night. Light snow has started to fall and the city looks like a picture postcard. I'm aching with the need to stay here and ask questions I need answered and to be with other people who are like me. But I finally get a cab and head back to the hotel.

Todd is waiting for me when I get to the hotel. "Where the hell have you been?"

"I did some sight-seeing; we can do more tonight."

"That might be fun," he muses, "but let's not make it a late night. I'm really tired."

"How was the school?"

He shrugs. "Pretty good, but I guess the only way to really know is to go there." Then he smiles. "Are you hungry?"

"Starved," I say, and we choose a restaurant from the guide the hotel has provided.

We hail a cab and hurl through the traffic to the restaurant we've chosen. Todd looks so handsome in the dim restaurant light. He wears a navy blue jacket with a dress shirt and tie.

"After we eat, we'll look around," he says. "There are lots of art galleries in Greenwich Village."

"Where's that?" I say, feigning innocence.

"You wouldn't know if I told you. But there are lots of things to see there."

After dinner, we get back into a cab and head for the Village. Snow has covered the streets and it feels like we're on another planet.

Then Todd gives me this wise little smile. "You may be intimidated by the Village," he says, "because it's basically a gay community. Because there are so many gays here, they have a sense of community and openness missing for gays in smaller places."

It's my turn to smile. "Perhaps we'll find Coach Wheeler here."

Todd and I start our tour by looking into some small shops. One shop in particular draws my attention. Huge, wooden, carved pieces decorate the windows. We go inside for a closer look. Some of the wooden statues are taller than we are, and they are intricately carved.

A pair of statues catches my eye—they signify man and woman, roughly carved and misshapen. The man who owns the shop explains that they are fertility statues, symbols of an ancient African tribe.

Being in the shop gives me the feeling of being a part of another world. If these statues could speak, they would tell us of ways of life that are totally unknown to me.

We walk the streets a long while, pausing to look in different windows. One shop has a full line of punk-rock clothing. "The price tags are even more outrageous," says Todd.

We look at a shirt that's embossed with silver threads: thirty-five dollars. "I bet it isn't even wash-and-wear," I say, and we both laugh.

Young men pass us on the streets as we walk and I wonder what they are thinking. Do they think that Todd and I are lovers? In this place, that's the norm.

Todd's favorite places are the shops that have prints and lithographs. After carefully searching through several shops, he buys a print and the shopkeeper carefully rolls it into a tube.

"Want to see a movie or a play?" Todd asks. We consider what is playing. The streets are lined with small playhouses and in front of one, Todd stops short.

"This looks like a fun play," he says.

I'm amazed to read the title: *Boy Meets Boy*.

"It's kinda like when in Africa, do as the Africans do," Todd explains. "Perhaps this play will give us a little insight."

Most of the audience is male. Todd stretches out his legs. He looks far more at ease than I do.

Several of the men are holding hands, but Todd seems almost oblivious to it. "It's just another lifestyle, Mike," he says. "In some countries, it's an accepted life-style—the Africans often have affairs with their own sex. So do the Greeks."

I wonder where and when Todd became so knowledgeable on this subject. The play is a musical and it's great—full of bright, witty moments and love and laughter. When it draws to a close and the two male characters marry, you feel that's the right ending. Todd enjoys it, too.

"I loved it," he says. "Weren't the songs great?"

As we are walking from the theater, Todd turns to me. "Don't tell your mom I took you to a gay play, okay?"

"I won't. She'd use it as a jumping-off point for yet another long lecture. Sometimes I pray she'll get laryngitis."

Todd yawns and stretches. "God, I'm so tired. How about you?"

Going to bed is the last thing on my mind. I want to explore, to learn, to feel. "No, I'm not," I say truthfully.

"Would you mind winging it on your own?" Todd asks. "I think I want to go back to the hotel to sleep."

Do I mind? I'm delighted. As the red lights of his cab speed away, I try to remember the directions to the piano bar.

I hear the music and the sound of singing voices before I even realize this is the bar. Several steps down, there's a dimly lit room with a piano. People stand around it singing and holding mugs of beer. There are lots of girls there, something I hadn't counted on. The guy from the ice cream store is there and he waves at me across the room. "Hi, Mike. Over here."

He smiles as I approach, then he hugs my shoulders and kisses me. So many people here kiss when they meet. I think it's great, but it still feels strange. The newness must show on my face and by the way I stiffen. He doesn't notice and he puts his arm around my shoulder. I feel great. I order a beer and no one even questions my age.

"Just sing along," Jan says, and I do. I feel better than I have in the past year. I feel like I belong.

"Are you new here?" a heavyset girl asks.

I smile at her. "I live in New Jersey."

She gives me a wide grin. "We've been hearing rumors that people live there, and you're proof that it's inhabited. So you're a Jerseyan?"

Time passes quickly and at one point Jan smiles at me and asks if I'd like to go back to his apartment with him.

"Sure," I say bravely, "that might be fun."

My heart is in my throat. What will he expect? Will we have coffee and talk? Or will there be more? As we slowly walk down the snowy streets, he keeps his arm around my shoulder in a protective way. He opens a small hallway door and then he fumbles for his key.

"Try that one," I suggest and suddenly he presses against me and gives me a long, hard, kiss.

Fear rises in me, like a wave during a storm. I push him away. "I can't do this," I say, hearing the edge of tears in my own voice, and hating myself for it. "I guess I'm just not ready now. My friend will be worried about where I am."

"Don't be like this," Jan says in a half pleading voice. Then he takes my hands and pushes them into his jacket pockets.

"I said I can't." My voice is almost a cry now. I open the door and run out into the snow.

I run until my chest hurts when I try to breathe. I welcome the hurting. "Cab! Cab!" I call, and a yellow cab with a checkered roof pulls to the side of the street. Tears are running down my face as I climb inside.

The driver gives me a look of concern: "You okay, kid?"

"I'm fine," I say. During the ride, I try to calm myself. When I get out near the hotel I stand outside and lift my face skyward. The snow is falling steadily and it cuts my face as it lands. It's not a soft snow, but a mixture of rain and snow. The lights give it an eerie effect and for a moment I can imagine that I'm in another dimension.

It's been a strange night. I feel that the old me has died and left everything behind him. Where do I fit into all of this? Will my life be spent in hallways with quick, furtive kisses and hugs? Or will I someday be comfortable enough with the knowledge of who I am to be able to love in the open?

Upstairs, Todd is asleep on the sofa. The television flickers mutely with a test pattern. I wish he would wake up and hold me close and tell me everything will be okay. I cover him with a sheet, feeling overcome with tender feelings for him. Feelings I know that I will have to bury forever.

That night my dreams are bizarre. I am alone in a snowstorm and I keep beating on a door. No one comes and finally my hands are frozen. My feet ache with a pain I've never before imagined. I keep beating and beating on the door until my blood colors the snow. People look out their windows and see me, but they won't let me inside. I realize that the people are my family.

I must be screaming in real life as well as in my dream, for I waken to find Todd standing over me, a puzzled look on his face.

"Wake up, Mike," he says. "You keep yelling for someone to let you in. You're gonna wake up the whole hotel."

Oh, God, what a nightmare. The images are still fresh in my mind. "It was awful. It was so cold and I was banging on the door and my family wouldn't let me in," I say. The fear inside me from the dream is still so real.

Todd grins broadly. "It's because you didn't clean your room," he jokes, "and your mom says you'll stay out in that snow until you do."

Suddenly his smile fades and he looks at me with the earnestness that's so much a part of him. "Mike, is something bothering you? If there is, please tell me. Between us, we can work it out."

I do want to tell Todd. Perhaps more than anything else in the world. I want to tell him about this dark secret I've been holding in.

I want to tell him about Jan and what happened last night.

He sits, waiting, his blue eyes locked with mine. I freeze. The words won't come. "I guess I had too much to drink."

"Mike, there's more." Todd is not so easily dismissed. "We've been friends since first grade. I know you well enough to know that something is eating at you. And, man, you are being eaten up. Tell me! What are best friends for, anyway?"

I change the subject and soon the early morning discussion is forgotten. "Let's finish our Christmas shopping," Todd suggests. We pull out our lists and head for the stores.

Macy's is our first choice. It looks like fairyland. The windows have small mechanical figures that bring the Christmas theme to life.

"I want to get Dee a friendship ring," Todd says, so we search the jewelry department for just the right ring. The salesgirl flirts with us and tries on each ring we choose.

"She sure is a lucky girl," the salesgirl says.

"Let me see the one with the little hearts on it." Todd makes his selection. "That's pretty." He holds the ring in his hand, studying its intricate design. "What do you think?" He holds the ring up for me to look at.

"I think it's perfect. Dee will love it. I'm sure she will."

"Get one for Trisha too," Todd urges, but I beg off.

"I'd rather get her a book she said she wanted." A ring is the last thing I want to give to Trisha.

We buy the ring and then the book and I have it gift wrapped. Then I see a soft flannel nightgown that Trisha would love. Amidst lots of teasing from Todd, I buy it and have it wrapped.

"Flannel?" he jokes. "Flannel for a honeymoon?"

"No honeymoon yet, Todd. I hope to have a few more free years."

"Do you want to have kids?"

"Sure I do—someday," I say, feeling a bit depressed.

"Me too," says Todd. "You know, I can't wait for that. Little Todd, Jr. He'll be so tough. And so special. He'll be a cross between Dee and me, and that will make him a super kid."

He muses a moment. "I'd like him to be taller than me—and smarter, of course. Just look at who his mommy will be. How lucky can one kid get?" He seems lost in a fantasy world of wives and babies.

I'm sure the birth of Todd's first son will be a major occasion in my life. "Can I be the godfather?" I ask.

"Of course you'll be the godfather," Todd says. "Who else would be the godfather?"

The godfather, as I remember, has a lot of responsibility. When you know about me, Todd, will you still want me to be a guiding force in your son's life?

I know I'll always have children in my life—Steve's, Jeffie's, and Todd's. But I know with an inner certainty that I'll never have a child of my own. I grieve a little for that lost child. It would be nice to share the birth experience with someone—the waiting, the actual birth, the final realization that you have added a touch of immortality to this world.

I can't even allow myself to think about this stuff. To even consider doing it would be unfair to the child and his mother. I could never love a woman fully, in the way she needs to be loved. If I tried, I'd be responsible for messing up a lot of lives.

Todd will have to have the sons. And like Jeff Hart, before me, I will be the doting godfather, with a godchild like Jeffie to spoil.

Our time in New York ends too soon. We board the bus that will take us home and I almost feel like I'm going to cry as the bus edges its way into the Lincoln Tunnel. I straighten up my act fast, before Todd assumes I've gone over the edge.

"What's the matter?" He eyes me suspiciously. "The smoke in the tunnel getting to you?"

I force a cough and rub both eyes with balled-up fists. "I think I'm allergic to this air."

When the bus pulls into the depot at home, Trisha and Dee are waiting for us.

"Oh, Mike." Trisha hugs me close. "I've missed you so much." From the corner of my eye, I see Todd and Dee all wrapped up in each other's arms. Trisha eyes the shopping bags. "What'd ya do? Buy out the stores?"

Todd's face is beaming as he slaps me on the back. "Isn't it great to be home?" I think I want to cry.

Later, when we're alone, Trisha gives me the third degree. "Did you meet any nice girls in the city?" I have this crazy desire to blurt out the truth. To watch her face grow pale as I say, "No, Trish, but you should see this wonderful guy named Jan that I met."

But I don't really even consider it. I just smile and assure her that no other girl could ever take her place.

CHAPTER THIRTEEN

"SO HOW was the city?" Steve looks up at me from the bed where he has his nose buried in a book.

"It was great. We stopped and saw some art galleries and we visited Times Square and Greenwich Village."

"Lots of fags down there," Steve says. I'm shocked. Somehow I never expected that from him. "Did any of them try to flirt with you or Todd?"

"No," I say quietly. I had considered telling Steve before anyone else. Now I have second thoughts about it.

"We had one of them living in our building at school," Steve says, "and he always wore dresses when he went out at night. Carole loved him, they were like girl friends, trading recipes and shopping together. I could never understand why she liked him so much. In fact, it was one thing we fought about a lot."

Maybe Carole was right in getting rid of Steve.

"Maybe he was a nice person," I argue. "I'm sure he had something to offer or Carole wouldn't have liked him so much."

"He was okay at times, but when I saw him in that dress it was all over. Queer is queer. There's no changing that."

"Most gays don't wear dresses."

Steve looks at me strangely. "What are you, an authority on the gay world because you took one trip to Greenwich Village? Fags are all the same—I know. Believe me, you can spot one a mile away."

I smile to myself and think, Oh yeah? That's what you think, big brother.

I don't want to argue with him and I stop the conversation because Jeffie has entered the room and is rummaging through my suitcase.

"Did you bring me a surprise?" he asks, jumping up and down on my bed.

Steve tells him to be quiet. "You think anytime anyone goes anyplace you should get something?"

Jeffie's face looks sad, so I pull out the small box of candy that I bought for him. It's chocolate in the shape of little elves and I'm sure it reminds him of his play.

He hugs and kisses me with wet, loud kisses. "Thanks, Mike, you're a good brother." He gives a down-the-nose glance at Steve that says *And you're not such a good brother*. Then he takes his candy and is gone.

"You all spoil that kid," Steve complains. "He's gonna grow up to be a real brat."

"Oh, Steve," I argue, "Jeffie's a good kid." He just ignores me and goes back to his book.

Steve has changed so much since he's been home. Sometimes I look at him and wonder where the real Steve has gone. Perhaps that's what your first real heartache does to you. Or perhaps it's just getting older.

Dad wants to hear about my trip. I tell him how we really got to see New York and I tell him about the art galleries. "Some of the works we saw there are beautiful," I say. "Maybe someday you and I can go to New York."

Dad looks pleased. "I'd really like that, Mike."

Then he smiles at me. "I took your advice and started to draw again. Come upstairs with me and I'll show you some of the stuff I've done."

We climb the stairs to Mom and Dad's room. Dad opens his desk drawer and takes out a large sketch pad. He flips it open and hands it to me.

My dad is a great artist. There's Jeffie hugging Grouch—the drawing looks as good as a photograph. There's one of Grouch stretched out on the table and one of Mom when she was younger. Her hair is framing her face in wispy little curls.

"That's how I always see your mother," Dad explains. "She was always so pretty and her hair always fell in little curls around her face."

"How do you like this one?" Dad flips the page and my own likeness smiles back at me. I'm wearing my soccer jersey and my hair is tousled. "You favor Mom," he says. "I guess that's why I've always had special feelings about you."

I get a lump in my throat. I never realized we looked alike, but looking at the drawings, I can see it.

"You're the unusual one," Dad tells me. "You look like Mom, but you act like me. Steve and Jeff have a certain boldness that comes from Mom. They can face things and bounce back without too much pain. But you're like me—more sensitive. Things go deeper with you. They bother you and you have to work at sorting them out."

Dad is right about that. I always take everything to heart. If a teacher yells at the whole class, I always assume she's yelling at me.

"Sensitive people have a hard time of it," Dad says, "but in the long run, they learn so much more because they care enough about other people to look deeper than the surface."

I'm enjoying this conversation with Dad. It's all too seldom that we get to talk like this.

"Want to take a ride with me?" he asks. "I'm taking the sketches over to show Jeff Hart. He just called and said that he'll be in town for the next few days. I know he'll try to get the one of Jeffie away from me. He considers that kid his property because he's the godfather."

I'm glad that Dad has asked me to go. I've been waiting for a chance to get a close look at Jeff, now that I know he's gay.

I go back into my room and put my jacket on. "Where are ya goin'?" Steve looks up from his book.

"With Dad to see Jeff Hart," I say, and Steve mumbles at me to have a good time, then buries his nose back into his book.

"I'll be glad to see Jeff," Dad says as we pull into the parking lot of the Holiday Inn. "It's been awhile since we got together."

We ask at the desk for his room number and then get into the elevator for the long ride to the tenth floor. On the way up Dad gives me an earnest look. "You won't be uncomfortable, will you," he asks, "because I told you that Jeff is homosexual?"

I smile. "Of course not, Dad. Jeff is like an uncle to me. Why would that change my feelings?"

Dad smiles at me. "I'm pleased with the way you think, Mike."

Jeff greets us at the door and encompasses us both in a hug. "God, Mike, you're all grown up."

He appraises me, then smiles. "You look a lot like your mom."

"Thanks," I say, smiling back at him. "That's what Dad says, too."

I sit on the small couch in the room and watch the interaction between my dad and Jeff. They've been friends a long time, they've shared so much. The fact that Jeff is gay doesn't seem to matter at all in their relationship. For one thing, I notice that Dad is a lot more open with Jeff than he is with his other male friends. They hug and touch as they speak. And neither of them is uncomfortable.

Dad looks at me and gestures. "By the way, Jeff, I hope you don't mind, but Mike and I were discussing homosexuality and I told him you're gay."

Jeff's smile becomes a little defensive. "So how did you take that news, Mike?"

I give him a smile, meant to be wide. "I think it's interesting."

"Most kids today are more knowledgeable on the subject, but when I was your age being gay was a total social disaster."

I feel like telling him it still isn't easy, even in the enlightened 1980s—there are still plenty of people who make judgments and throw stones. There are people who would have men like Jeff and me thrown in jail if they could. And for what? For loving someone. Killers go free these days, and everyone has their right to be heard and tried fairly. Except men like you and me, Jeff. But instead I say, "Perhaps people are a little more liberated, but there's still a lot of misunderstanding."

"You can say that again," Jeff says. I notice that he is a very handsome man. My dad, who is the same age, has a little potbelly and he doesn't take as much care with his appearance as Jeff does. Jeff is impeccably groomed and his clothes look as if they were designed by his own special tailor.

"One time I was working at this straight bar for a few months and every time I turned around the conversation was about homosexuality. No one there knew I was gay and most of the time they talked so badly about gays that I wanted to scream. But I couldn't. I had to stay quiet or risk losing my job. I had to listen to how faggots molest little boys and chase straight men and how they all wear dresses and really are women in men's bodies. I had to listen—and perhaps having to listen was worse because I wanted so much to be able to say that it wasn't true. I don't know if it's harder to face up to being gay or to keep quiet and listen to all of the jokes and ridicule. I know that after a few months I had to quit that job. I felt like I was going crazy."

He seems happy to be able to talk about it. "So many people are ignorant," he says, "and sometimes I'm so hurt inside that I wish I could die and get it over with. I've always wondered why this happened to me. Why couldn't I have been like 80 percent of the world—totally straight? But then I wonder if I would have been happy that way either. Now homosexuality is more out in the open. But there still is a cloud that surrounds it. I think the fact that people only speak of it in whispers has something to do with it. If all the mystery and mystique were erased, everyone would see that I'm exactly the same as they are, but that I happen to prefer men sexually."

"Did you tell your parents?" I may as well learn it all.

"Yes, I did. My mother cried and went to bed for a week. My father threatened to kill me. Then they both suggested I see a therapist because obviously I needed some therapy. They weren't willing to accept me as a gay person. They were put off by it. Even after my mother sort of accepted it, she made me feel guilty about being gay. She used to caution me never to let anyone know about it. How do you think that made me feel? The period of time after I told them was the worst time of my life. I felt if they couldn't accept me—my own parents—how could anyone else?"

"Do you have a lover?" I can't believe I've asked that and I feel my face flush a deep red.

Jeff laughs at me. "Don't blush, Mike. I've had a series of lovers. But unfortunately I've never seemed to be able to find a perfect mate, the way your dad did." He pauses a moment. "I want you to know, Mike, that your dad is a prince of a man. When we were in school and all of the other guys were calling 'faggot,' your dad remained my best friend. It wasn't easy for him either, because once the other guys knew, they started making innuendos. But he didn't care. That's what it means to be a man of principle. Your dad happens to be one of the best men in the world.

"God, for a long time, I had the biggest crush on him, but I knew it could never work. He was straight. I always knew that and I respected him for it. But he was the most decent human being I knew. So I loved him. I never told him in the beginning, but I'm sure he knew it. Even today, he's my closest friend."

How ironic, I think. Todd and I are like history repeating itself.

Perhaps some day in the future, I will be saying these same things to Todd's son. I feel better knowing Dad is so accepting. Maybe it will make it easier to tell him I'm gay.

Dad shows Jeff his drawings and, as he predicted, Jeff demands to be given the one of Jeffie and Grouch. Dad grumbles a little but he tears the drawing from the book and gives it to Jeff.

The three of us decide we can use a late evening snack so we go to the fancy little dining room at the Holiday Inn. The waitress is funny and she tells jokes as she serves our sandwiches. "I don't know when I've seen three such good-looking guys," she says, "each one more handsome than the next."

I wonder if I am handsome. For some reason I can see my flaws more easily than I can see my good qualities. But other people always tell me I'm good-looking.

After our snack, we head home. Dad says, "I love the way you handled yourself tonight, Mike. It showed real maturity."

I smile at my dad and I want to tell him that tonight was more for me than it was for him. For the first time I feel a real identity with my dad, and hence with myself.

CHAPTER FOURTEEN

"HELP ME wrap, Mike." Jeffie is enmeshed in a tangle of paper, tape, and bows. He is doing his annual wrap-a-thon for Christmas. He enjoys the whole concept of giving. I notice one of his favorite toys, a robot, in the pile of gifts to be wrapped.

"Who is this for?"

"It's for you and Todd to take to the kids at the home," he says. "They might really like him. He's a good robot."

"He sure has been." I pinch Jeffie's nose.

He does a little dance and smiles at me. "Will you and Trisha take me to the animals and the baby?" Our town has a live nativity and it's one of the prettiest I've seen anyplace.

"Sure, we're planning on it—maybe later today," I tell him. As he wraps, he mutters to himself. He always takes too much tape off the roll and then it gets stuck to itself. So by the time he's finished, it's almost as if he's the present—all wrapped in tape.

"What are you guys doing?" Mom calls.
Jeffie hurriedly pushes her gift under the bed. "Stay away," he yells. "It's a secret."

Mom puzzles me. Maybe she's missing something in life, but she tries to hold on to us so tightly. I know what she feels is genuine love and concern, but there are times when I want to tell her to just let me try my wings. I guess Steve and I are lucky there is a Jeffie. Otherwise, Mom would be even more clingy.

We're about halfway through the wrapping when Trisha appears. She hugs me and then gives Jeffie a peck on the cheek. "Let's go get a soda," she suggests. "Then we could take the kid here to see the nativity."

Jeffie pushes the rest of the stuff under his bed. "Sure, I'm ready." He runs out to get his jacket and mittens. Mom insists he wash his face and he grumbles as he does it.

The streets are coated with snow. Jeffie beams. "Santa won't have a bit of trouble now," he chortles. He makes snowballs and tries to hit Trisha and me but finally I bury him in a snowbank. "Now, knock it off," I threaten, "or you won't make it any farther than the ice cream parlor."

At the store, Jeffie draws his usual crowd of admirers. All of the girls ooh and ahh over him, and they all want to buy him something. The little opportunist lets them. In fact, he usually leads them to the candy counter while he decides what pleases him. But he has such a cute personality that people love him. I should be as popular as that midget.

After he's had his fill of the girls, he stands up. "Lets go see the manger," he says, "before it gets too late."

We walk to the church, where cattle, camels, and lambs walk around. The small manger scene is full of people: a woman in a blue robe, a man with a beard who looks very concerned, and an infant with waving arms who moves restlessly on his straw bed.

Jeffie is enthralled. His eyes sparkle as he reaches out to touch the nose of a baby goat. The goat sniffs his mittens for a moment then starts to nibble on them. Jeffie laughs. "Hey, goat, this isn't your breakfast, ya know."

Within a few moments it appears that Jeffie and the goat are bosom buddies.

"Let's go see the baby," I suggest, and Jeffie takes my hand. Together we walk to the manger and I kneel down and balance Jeffie on my knee. The snow is falling in large flakes and some of them have stuck to Jeffie's hat. As he looks at the baby his eyes become serious. "Isn't the baby Jesus cute?" I ask him, feeling for all the world like a father.

Jeffie regards the baby with solemn eyes. He goes to Sunday School, so I guess at this time of the year this is the story they are learning.

"He's God's son," he whispers.

"Well, this baby isn't," I say, "but Jesus was."

"We are all God's sons," he corrects me.

"You two are so serious," Trisha says. "You sound like a teacher and pupil, but I'm not sure which of you is the teacher."

I pick up Jeffie and he hugs me suddenly. His small sturdy body feels good in my arms.

We pick up some straw and hold it out to the sheep and one of them starts to nibble on it. That sends Jeffie into delighted shrieks.

We walk over to the Santa Claus booth and Jeffie climbs right up on his knee. "Hi, Santa."

Santa smiles. "Have you been good?"

Jeffie is honest. He pauses a moment, removes his woolen cap, and scratches his head. "Well, sometimes I'm not."

Santa obviously isn't used to hearing this. He tries again: "Well are you usually good?"

Jeffie screws up his face. "I usually try to be good." That's all he can manage. Santa winks at me. "That's all old Santa can ask for—for you to try to be good. What do you want?"

I lean back and prepare to listen to a list that's ten miles long. Jeffie grows serious. "I want my brother Steve to be able to live with Carole again," he says.

Santa knows he's dealing with a special kid. He doesn't try to talk him out of what he's feeling. He scratches his head. "I'd love to be able to do that, but how would you suggest I go about it?"

Jeffie's eyes open wide. "I don't know. I've thought about it a lot. If you can't help, I guess there's no hope."

"There's always hope," Santa says, "as long as you're around." He gives Jeffie a lollipop and tells him he'll try to help.

I see the parents milling around the area with their children and again I feel a sense of loss for the children I will never have. But I've learned a lesson—a child doesn't have to be yours for you to love it. We walk home and drop Trisha off on the way.

"Jeffie, you're a hoot," she tells him.

He looks up at me. "Is that good, Mike?" he asks. "Is it good to be a hoot?"

Todd comes over later to do some last-minute shopping. I tell him about Jeffie and Santa Claus. He seems moved. "That kid is one in a million," he says. "By the way, Mike, are you finished with your shopping?"

"Most of it," I say, "at least the major stuff. I still have a few things to get, but for the most part, I'm finished."

"This Christmas will be hard because of Gran. She was such a big part of the holiday. She used to bake hundreds of cookies and both she and her house smelled like gingerbread for weeks before the holiday. That's one reason why Christmas won't feel the same this year."

He looks so sad. I wish I could hug him and tell him that these feelings will pass, but at this moment we are both far too straight for that to happen. We haven't even had a beer—there's no excuse for physical closeness. I let it slide.

"I'll miss Carole this Christmas," I say. "She's been at the house at Christmas for so many years that it will seem weird without her."

"There have been so many changes this year. It seems like we're always making changes."

That's what life is all about, I guess. It has been a year of change, of growth, and of loss. A year to think about for many years to come.

CHAPTER FIFTEEN

STEVE IS reading when I walk into the room. He looks up and asks, "Do you think Carole will ever want to go back with me? I know she spoke to you the last time she was here."

"I don't know, Steve. Maybe the two of you are on different wavelengths. Sometimes love grows in different directions."

"You're so old and jaded for sixteen," Steve says. "Sometimes I feel like I'm the kid brother."

Lately all of Steve's niceness has been erased by his depression. There are days when I feel like grabbing him by the shirt and pushing him out of the house and out of my life. There's still a whole big world out there that Steve won't even look at. But obviously Steve's world has been Carole for so long that without her there's a big void.

I wish I could talk to Steve about my problem because he usually has good sense about things. Now is not the time. He's too preoccupied with Carole and he's made his views on gay people all too clear.

That night I lie awake a long time, way past the time when Steve's even breathing signifies he's asleep. I wonder what life was like for Jeff Hart when he was my age. And I wonder if Todd will be as understanding as my dad was, when I tell him. It's funny. Lately when I've thought about Todd it's "when I tell him," not "if I tell him." I know deep within me that this is something we two will have to share at some point. But I'll have to be ready for it when it comes. Todd's reaction may not be favorable. Maybe I give him too much credit.

I'm a careful person for a Gemini. Usually Geminis aren't that cautious, but I try to plan everything I do down to the last detail. I always consider all alternatives before I act. Mom always teases me because she's a Gemini too and she never thinks about anything. She just sort of plunges into things, but she's been lucky because they usually work for her.

I toss and turn and decide I can't sleep. So I put my earphones on and listen to some music. I put my bedside light on and look through some old scrapbooks. I call it a nostalgia run.

There's Trisha when I first knew her. She's about eleven and very shy. She stands in this gawky pose with a cross-eyed look, clowning around in front of the camera. Looking at that picture brings out tender feelings in me—Trisha was so insecure at that time. Her teeth had braces on them and she was skinny as a pole. She was taller than most of the other kids in the class, including me. Then Trisha stopped growing and the rest of us caught up and passed her.

Her pixie face is dwarfed by two long pigtails that hang to her waist. Trish never had her hair cut until she was in the eighth grade. Her mother loved it long and Trisha was always too afraid to voice her opinion. But in the eighth grade she had a fight with her mom and snipped off the pigtails. Her mother still cries if Trisha talks about it.

There's a snapshot of Todd and me. We both have Band-Aids on our knees and Todd is wearing his cowboy hat. He wore that hat every day for years. It seemed like it was part of his head. Finally his mom managed to hide it and it didn't show up again for about three years. When it did show up, we were thirteen and Todd laughed at himself. "No wonder Mom hid it," he said. "It really was stupid-looking."

There's a picture of Todd with a newborn Margaret Ann in his arms. Todd looks scared to death and the baby's face is a blur. He was so sure that he would get a brother that he cried when his dad told him she was a girl.

There are clippings about plays we were in. Also, the usual memorabilia that one collects through grammar school days, like a faded newspaper print of me and a cow. We'd visited a farm and when she licked my face, someone took a picture of it.

There's a picture of Steve and me in red plaid jackets, sitting on the knee of the Macy's Santa Claus one year. I'm missing some teeth. There we sit, like two little boys anywhere in America. Every family has to have a picture like this one.

Mom has a special box of memorabilia—first teeth, baby shoes, the candles from our first birthday cakes. She is very sentimental. Dad is sentimental too, but he shows it in different ways. Every Christmas he patiently stood and took home movies of the event. He shows them every Christmas, for tradition's sake. Every single reel has Steve and I twisting and waving for the camera. And later on, the infant Jeffie—Mom's surprise package, she called him at first.

In my book I have the first photos ever taken of Jeffie. Jeff Hart had given me a camera for my birthday and Jeffie was born around that time. He made me promise to send him a lot of pictures of his new godson. I think I sent pictures three times, but then the camera broke.

In so many ways I'm just like everyone else—why do I always feel so different?

God, do I need someone to talk to. For a moment I toy with the idea of telling Jeff Hart, but then I change my mind. That wouldn't be wise. Then suddenly I make a decision. I'm going to tell Todd.

First I have to set a date to tell him. I make a project of that. What date would be appropriate? I decide the Fourth of July would have to be the time. That gives me time to plan it. Independence day. Once I tell Todd, I will be free from the invisible chains that tie my soul down. But I know I have to prepare for something else, too. If Todd reacts the wrong way, it may take me years to recover from it. I feel better. On July fifth, the whole thing will be over. That means I'll have about six months to worry about it.

I wake up the next morning with a feeling of peace. I have set my goal and I'll follow through with it.

The week is full of social events. Everyone, it seems, is having a party. We eat, drink, and be merry until my belt is getting hard to buckle. Todd and I spend the last few nights before Christmas shopping for last-minute gifts. I'm happy that I've saved enough money from summer jobs to get Dad a wonderful set of paints.

Christmas Eve is all snowy and beautiful. I think that of all the special times, Christmas Eve is my favorite. It's a time when everyone has tender feelings for his fellow man. No one is mean. Everyone is full of the joy of the season.

As usual we plan a family party for the early evening that will end with a midnight trip to church.

I am basically a religious person. I have deep beliefs and although I don't go to church regularly, I am spiritual in my own way.

Mom has been cooking all day, Jeffie is bursting with excitement, and Steve is happier because Carole called to wish us all Happy Holidays. He seems to be accepting the loss of Carole a little more. This evening he surprises us with a dinner guest named Naomi.

"Naomi is Jewish," he announces. "She's never celebrated Christmas."

Naomi has wide brown eyes that look like a deer's and her hair is a mass of curls. She smiles a lot. I get good vibrations from her.

Trisha arrives, her arms full of packages. Jeffie busies himself poking through them, reading the labels.

The most special gift I'm giving is, of course, for Todd. I shopped a long time to find just the right thing and I think I've managed to find it.

When Todd was small, he got lost and a policeman found him. He tried to find out who Todd was, but Todd was having so much fun riding in the police car and eating ice cream cones that he wouldn't tell them his name. It went on for five hours before he finally let them in on who he was. So for Todd, I found a Norman Rockwell print of a little boy and a police officer. They are sitting in the stationhouse, eating ice cream, and the cop is questioning the child. I'm sure it will make Todd laugh.

For Trisha there is a nightgown, several small pieces of jewelry, and a book. She has hinted about a ring, but I try to ignore that.

For Mom there's also a special book she wanted, and for Jeffie, I splurged and bought an electric raceway. I know I'll regret it because he'll be after me to play with him. For Steve, I found an old Truman Capote first edition.

The evening is beautiful. We eat at my house then go to Trisha's, then to Todd's, then to Dee's. By the time we are ready for church, I feel so stuffed that

I can hardly walk. The four of us walk through the powdery snow to the church where Todd and I attended Sunday School.

"We used to be in the choir," Todd says. "We wore little red gowns and little red hats. Mike was always getting yelled at for chewing bubble gum."

A mental picture flashes back to me. Todd and I are both ten, looking very reverent. Our hair is brushed and shiny under our choir caps. The music is filling the church and we hold our hymnals and sing like little robins. Then I start to blow a bubble. Instead of breaking like it usually does, the bubble grows and grows until it fills the whole front of my face. Suddenly a hymnal crashes into my head, and the bubble bursts all over my face. I turn around to the glaring face of the old choir director. I want to cry, I'm so embarrassed. Todd is giggling into his hands. *Gloria in excelsis . . . amen.*

Tonight, the church smells of holly and pine. Candles light up every window and in the front of the church the manger holds a newborn child. Our church always has a live nativity on Christmas Eve.

I walk to the nativity scene and kneel beside the manger. The baby in the manger stops squirming and looks up at me. Suddenly, a wave of guilt washes over me. Oh, little babe, will you be able to understand that I am still spiritual, still in touch with religion, even though I'm gay? Todd and Dee are smiling at the baby as it grabs for Trisha's finger. I touch the smooth little leg that extends from the blanket.

I know for certain that Jesus will not judge me. He loves people too much to judge me for something I can't help. I am secure in that knowledge.

CHAPTER SIXTEEN

"NEW YEAR'S EVE," I say into the mirror as I knot the tie Mom picked out for Jeffie to give me for Christmas. "Thank God for tradition."

Every New Year's Eve since I can remember, we've gone over to Todd's house for a party. It started the year Todd and I became friends—our parents used the occasion to get to know each other better. Todd's mom invited my parents to their house for a quiet two-family celebration. Over the years many other people have been included, so now it's one of the nicest open-house parties of the year for all of us. I'm sure this year will be no exception.

"Mike," Dad yells, "hurry or you'll be late to pick up Trisha."

"Coming." I pick up my jacket from the bed and take one more quick look in the mirror. I still look the same, I reassure myself, as I've done every day for months now. All this craziness inside of me and I still look the same.

Driving over to Trisha's I have a chance to think about tonight. Not only about the party, but about tonight being a night of changes. It's a new year and to start it off Todd says he and Dee are going to make love.

Trisha and I haven't made love in months now. But Todd really has his heart set on it. He loves Dee so much and she loves him too, so why shouldn't they? I'm glad that there hasn't been a good moment for Trisha and I to make love, because I don't know how I'd react. What would happen if I couldn't do it? That would give Trisha even more reason to wonder about what's happening with me.

"This is a wonderful party, Mrs. Davis," Dee says as she sips her champagne.

I watch the interaction between the two because they've never met before tonight. I know Mrs. Davis always liked Marcy, but she seems impressed with Dee. Of course, everyone is—she's such a special person.

Everyone, that is, except Trisha. We still argue about this relationship of Todd's because Marcy is still Trisha's best friend and Trisha thinks Todd owes something to Marcy.

Then there's the date I took Dee on. Trisha never misses a chance to rub that one in.

Trisha watches Mrs. Davis and Dee, too. "I bet she doesn't like Dee," she says. "Todd's mother really liked Marcy."

I feel like being a bastard. "Dee is prettier." I wonder how long it will take for Marcy to hear that one.

Todd is very nervous and when we're alone in his room, he asks my advice.

"Do you think we're makin' a mistake?" he asks.

I want to say yes, but I know that would be wrong. "Are you sure you love her?" I ask.

He nods. "I think I do. I've never felt this way before. Not with Marcy, that's for sure."

"Well then, have fun." My heart is heavy. I'm wishing for all the world that I could be spending the night with him.

"How about you and Trisha. Do you do it?" He catches me off guard. I laugh—my best offhanded laugh. "Sure. Didn't you and Marcy?"

He flushes. "Yeah. But it wasn't the same. I didn't feel like I had to question everything before I did it with her."

He grows serious. "Dee's never made love before, I hope I'm not making a mistake."

During the course of the evening, I see Todd downing more than his share of champagne. Maybe he figures if he's drunk it will be easier.

I can't brush away the feelings of jealousy that I have. I've never been a jealous person, but I don't want to share Todd. Especially in such an intimate way. Dee will soon know him in a way I can never know him—it's not fair. So I try to make myself feel good, too.

Dad gives me a wary look as I down another can of beer. "Mike, you've had enough to drink," he says sternly in the tone that says *You might think you're grown-up but I still have the final say-so over you.*

"But it's New Year's Eve, Dad," I argue. I catch a note of whininess in my answer.

"I said you've had enough." Dad may be quiet, but he has a way of saying things that makes you know he means business.

At midnight everyone kisses and I make a big deal out of kissing Trisha. I hold her close to me for an extra long time and kiss her long and hard. But I want to cry. This isn't what I want. I want to be over on the other side of the room with Todd. Instead I walk over and give him a manly handshake. "Happy

New Year, pal." He is more relaxed and pulls me to him in a bear hug. "Happy New Year, Mike."

He drags me over to Dee. "Give my best pal a New Year's kiss," he orders and Dee obliges. New Year's Eve is always sad and I am overcome with a desire to cry. In the first hours of the new year, Todd is going to be making love to the person he loves most in the world. I suppose I could counter it by making love with Trisha, but the desire isn't there.

After the last drink is finished, I walk Trish home, feeling sad and empty. I kiss Trisha good night at her front door, then walk the rest of the way alone. The streets are deserted and I whistle as I walk. I want my life to be simple. Is that so much to ask for?

For the rest of the night, I think about Todd and Dee and what they're doing. It's almost dawn before I fall into a restless sleep.

The next day Steve asks me what's wrong. "You were tossing and turning all night. Are you having some sort of problem?"

Lately so many people keep asking me what's the matter. I'll have to work on being more cheery and sociable.

It's two in the afternoon before Todd makes an appearance. He face is ashen. He says he has a hangover.

Dad gives him his "older folk" look and says, "You'll have to learn not to overindulge."

"It was fun," Todd says, and we climb the stairs to my room. We close the door and fall on the beds.

"How was it?" I ask.

He blushes. "I couldn't do it." He stares at the ceiling and avoids my eyes. "She wanted to, but I couldn't do it."

I want to be sympathetic, but I'm glad.

Immediately I feel bad for feeling this way. I do want Todd to be happy.

"You shouldn't have drunk so much." I ruffle his hair. "See what happens when you do?"

"Don't tease me, Mike." His face is serious. "I wonder if it's a sign. Do you think things will ever be okay?"

So Todd has his worries, too. Not the same ones I have, but worries nonetheless.

Jeffie intrudes on this sober moment by bursting into the room. He dives onto the bed and wrestles with Todd. Then he jumps off and like a small tornado, he's gone.

"That's what I like about Jeffie," Todd says. "He's a man of few words."

"Margaret Ann is getting better too, isn't she?"

Todd smiles. "It's about time, but yes, she is."

"I always wanted a brother," Todd says. "And when she was born I was sick about it. When your mom had Jeffie, I kept begging my mother to try again and I never understood why she wouldn't."

"We can share Jeffie."

Todd laughs. "We already do, don't we?

"I wonder if perhaps I thought I'd hurt Dee. She's never done it before. What if something happened?"

"You read too many books. Everything will be fine. Don't you know this is the time of sexual liberation?"

"Don't believe it," Todd mutters. "Not for everyone. Really nice girls like Dee who haven't had any experience are still the same as girls a generation ago."

I don't understand Todd sometimes, but I lay it to the fact that he's so crazy in love with Dee. He thinks everything about her is different.

"Well, you can always try again. Trying's half the fun."

"Maybe for you." He sighs. "Sometimes I wish I was thirty-five, married, and settled down already. Being young isn't what it's cracked up to be."

I couldn't agree with him more. Many times I've wished that a magic time machine would whisk me to ten years from now. Most of the traumas would be over and my life would have a plan. Or maybe it wouldn't—maybe I'd be twenty-six and wishing a time machine would whisk me back to sixteen.

It's funny how we forget the bad things and remember the good things. I know there were so many times when I hated school, but looking back I tend to remember only the good times. I guess nature protects us that way.

With Todd it's the same way. Usually I remember only the good things. But if I really think about it, I can remember times when we hated each other. Times we were so mad that we punched each other and rolled around on the floor trying to kill one another. But when I think of Todd, I don't think of those times. I just think of the times we shared things, times when we were both happy.

Once we were even going to be blood brothers. We'd seen the whole ceremony in an old Huckleberry Finn movie and we decided that we had to be blood brothers. We got a needle from his mom's sewing kit, sterilized it on the stove and climbed to the tree house for the ceremony.

Todd squinted his eyes and wrinkled his nose and touched the point to his finger. No blood. He did the whole wind up again—still no blood. "It won't cut," he said simply. "Here, you try."

I took the needle and suddenly I felt queasy. "I don't think I can do it either," I said. "Let's use cherry juice instead."

So we picked some ripe red cherries and smeared our hands with the juice and then entwined our fingers. "We're blood brothers," Todd shouted.

"We really are," I screamed back.

I smile at Todd. "Do you remember when we became blood brothers?" I ask.

He smiles. "Yeah, both of us were too chicken to prick ourselves with the needle," he says.

"See? We weren't as dumb as Steve always says we were," I answer, and we both laugh for a long time.

"He was the dumb one. Remember when someone dared him to ride his bike off the dock and he did? He lost his new bike in the water. And your dad spanked him all the way home."

"We were definitely smarter," I agree, "and Jeffie is even smarter than we were."

By the time Todd leaves he feels better about the night before.

Trisha calls minutes after Todd leaves. She asks me what I'm doing tonight. "My mom and dad won't be home," she says, "and we haven't been alone in so long. I thought tonight might give us a chance to be together."

I gulp and my mind searches frantically for an excuse, but I can't come up with one in time. I hear myself saying, "See you later."

I think of all the jokes that men make about their wives and sex. They say their wives have every excuse in the world for not making love. I wonder if Trisha would believe I have a headache.

CHAPTER SEVENTEEN

"MIKE, it's Groundhog Day," Jeffie says, making a solemn pronouncement. Since he started first grade he's aware of special days like this one. "I guess he won't be seeing his shadow, will he?" Jeffie pouts a little. Outside the snow is falling and there are powdery little drifts everywhere.

"Well, if he can shovel his way out of his hole, he might be able to see his shadow," I tease. "But, Jeff, that's just a story."

He plants his feet wide apart and puts his hands on his hips. "No it isn't, Mike. My teacher told me."

Jeffie thinks his teacher is the world's biggest expert. Whatever she says is law.

"Mike," he says, putting his face almost next to mine—so close I can see the jelly smeared on his mouth, "I want it to be summer soon."

I can't say I disagree. "I'm with you, Jeff."

"Let's fool the groundhog." His blue eyes start to

sparkle. "We could put a tent over the groundhog hole."

"Jeff, there's more than one groundhog."

He frowns. "Oh, I thought there was only one of them."

Winter always gets to me by Groundhog Day. I start itching to see some green grass and to feel the warm sun on my face. If I was rich, I'd leave New Jersey on Groundhog Day and spend the rest of the winter on a Caribbean cruise. But in reality I—like the rest of the people here—must face the snow and ice until about April.

This past month I have become even more introspective. I've started to write my feelings down. Somehow, that helps me to clarify them. It's a neat way to sort out my thoughts.

I've even taken to writing poetry. That's something I never could have done a few years ago. But putting my feelings on paper makes me feel better about things. One night last week, Jeffie saw me writing and asked what I was doing.

"I'm writing," I said simply.

"Does that mean you are an author?"

I said that in some ways it meant I was an author.

"Like Shakespeare?"

Who ever thought a kid Jeffie's age would know about Shakespeare? He's really incredible.

One of the poems I write deals with my feelings about Todd. I call it "Frustration" and it goes like this:

> Sometimes when you smile at me, you make
> me want to cry.
> Sometimes when you hug me, I want to pull
> away.
> Sometimes when I hear your voice, I want it
> to be still.

Sometimes when we share secrets, I wish
there were none to share.
I think these feelings are born of frustration.
I want so much more than you are able to
give back to me.
So much more than you can ever imagine, I
want.
Will I ever be able to tell you of my secrets?
To share with you my own inner desires and
hopes and dreams?
The innermost parts of my own being that you
know nothing about?
If I can, then the frustration will fade and be
replaced by joy.

I read it over a few times and decide it isn't too bad. There are so many times when I want to shake Todd and tell him to stop being so insensitive to me, but then I realize he isn't aware of what's going on inside me. I don't know what I want from him anymore.

My relationship with Trisha is going downhill. One afternoon last week we discussed what was happening to us. Trisha had never looked prettier. Her hair was brushed back from her face and her eyes were as clear and blue as the sky. "What's wrong, Mike?" she asked.

I wanted to put it into words she might understand, but I couldn't. So I shrugged my shoulders and smiled at her. "I don't know, honey, but I know that something is the matter."

Tears welled up in her eyes and she pulled off her mittens and toyed with the ring on her finger. "I want it to work for us, Mike," she said. Suddenly we were hugging each other and crying. I know she deserves more than I can ever give her. I feel so guilty about staying with her when I know it's all just a charade for me.

Oh, Trisha, I'm sorry.

Jeffie and I walk through the snow, looking for a groundhog hole. It's useless. They're all snowed in. When we get back home, Carole is there. I'm really glad to see her.

"Mike!" she cries when she sees me. Then I'm wrapped in her arms and she's hugging me tight.

"How've you been?" I ask. "What a great surprise on a snowy day."

"I was in town on business and couldn't pass up a chance to see you all." She smiles at me, a smile that is unsure. "How is Steve?" she asks in a lower voice.

"He's a little better," I say honestly. "It took some time but he's finally coming around."

She smiles again, but it's a sad smile. "I'm so glad to hear that, Mike. I'm getting married this month."

The room swims. This really is the end. Carole is getting married to someone besides Steve. She really will never be my sister. Somehow I've held on to that hope, even after they broke up.

"That's great"—I force a smile—"but I'm sorry you'll never be my sister."

"I'll always be your sister, Mike, in the ways that really count."

She takes my arm. "Let's go someplace," she says. "I don't want to be here when Steve gets back."

I want to spend some time with her alone, so I smile at her. "Sounds good to me."

The two of us trudge through the snow to the malt shop. Halfway there, Carole hits me with a snowball. "I'll get you back," I vow, and like two little kids we throw snowballs and tumble in the snow until we're both exhausted.

Her face is bright red and she rubs her face with mitted hands. "God, I'm cold."

"Me too," I say, shivering.

The malt shop is deserted and we choose a table near the window. After we order we sit back to talk.

"Mike, is something bothering you?" she says, adding her name to the list of people who have already asked this question. Her eyes seem to look into my soul and I wonder for an instant if she knows.

For some reason I can't explain, I say, "Yes. I'd like to talk to you about it."

"Sure, Mike."

"But you can never tell anyone else, okay?"

"That goes without saying, Mike. Talk away. Your problem is safe with me."

I trust her totally. I'm not sure how she'll react to what I'm saying, but I hope she can give me some good advice. The words form a lump in my throat the size of a soccer ball. My eyes feel very hot and dry. How can I say this and make it sound okay?

"Mike, nothing is that bad," she says as she pushes my hair back from my face.

"Carole, I think I'm gay." There. I said it. There in the middle of the malt shop on Groundhog Day. The words are said and they aren't surrounded by sparks and trails of fire.

Carole looks puzzled for a brief moment then she stands up and hugs me. "So that's it," she says. "I've known for quite some time that something was bothering you, but I never quite knew what it was."

"Do you hate me now?" The words tumble out.

She looks at me with surprise. "Hate you?" She sounds incredulous. "How can I hate you? I love you. Your being gay doesn't change that one bit."

"So many people say bad things about gay people, I guess it's hard to believe anyone could still love me."

"Don't listen to any of them, Mike. They don't know what they're talking about."

"It's scary. I've never been with another guy, but I know how I feel. A lot of it has to do with Todd. I have feelings for him that are more than what I should have for a best friend. I want to be like everyone else, but I can't be. Sometimes I think I want to die. Can you imagine Mom knowing this? She'd really have something to bitch at me about then, wouldn't she? Dad would be hurt and think he failed me someplace. And Steve hates gays. He told me that. And how about Jeffie? Will he want his brother to be different? So many people are quick to call faggot and they don't even understand what it's all about." Tears are welling up in my eyes and the words I've kept inside for so long are gushing out nonstop. "If I could be straight, I would be. But I'm not. So what do I do about that?"

"What you have to realize," Carole says quietly and calmly, all the while holding tightly to my hand, "is that you are the same person you have always been. You are still Mike Ramsey. You aren't any better or any worse than you were before you made this discovery about yourself. Some people may want to make you think you're different, but don't believe them. Love is beautiful, no matter who shares it. That is the important thing for you to know and remember. Don't ever let anyone tell you that you are less than they are because you happen to be attracted to men. It simply isn't true. I know lots of gays. Lots of them are warm, wonderful people. You can't let your sexual preference alter your life. You have to keep it in the proper perspective. You have to understand that the ignorance of others is just that—ignorance. And you have to be able to see the great worth you have as a person, Mike."

The tears are running down my face and the waitress who brings our order stares at me, but I don't care. I just care that this person who has always meant so much to me understands. She still loves me as much as she ever did—even if I am gay.

She adds a word of caution. "You can't expect Todd

to be able to return your feelings," she says. "I don't think Todd is gay. His emotional makeup is different from yours and you must respect him as he must respect you. You can always be his good friend. Someday you'll meet the right person for you. You'll be ready for it when it happens. It's not wrong for you to love Todd—it's a compliment to love someone. It would only be wrong for you to expect him to be able to return the affection." She smiles at me. "Does anyone else know, Mike?"

I shake my head no. She says she's honored that I chose to talk to her first.

I manage a smile through my tears. "Thanks so much for listening, Carole, and for not making judgments."

She hands me a paper napkin and I wipe my face with it. "Steve may be upset at first, but give him time. He'll come to realize you're still the same little brother he always loved. He cares too much about you to let this affect your relationship."

I feel so close to Carole. We've shared an important moment.

"Mike, if you ever need someone to talk with, call me."

"You've made me look at myself in a different way," I tell her as we walk back through the snow, "and for the first time in a long while, I feel a little better about what's happening."

In that short space of sharing a lunch with Carole, I've made the first big step into the world of being myself.

Carole says she can't stay because she doesn't want to see Steve. I stand in the snow for a long time after the lights of her car fade into the distance. She's been gone about half an hour when Steve gets home.

Jeffie greets him at the door, hands full of lollipops. "Carole was here and she brought me these," he says, "and she took Mike for a burger."

Steve looks at me with eyes strangely dark. "Where is she now?"

"She had to leave."

We walk to the bedroom together. I have a feeling of pressure in my chest. How will I tell Steve that Carole is marrying? The news will break his heart, I'm sure.

We close the door of the room and he looks at me levelly. "Tell me everything, Mike. I have to know."

"She looks good," I say, hedging the issue. "She said to say hi. She bought me a burger."

"Tell me the real news." Steve won't be deterred.

"Carole is getting married," I say softly.

Tears fill his eyes but they don't overflow. He doesn't say a word. He turns on his reading light and picks up a book. Although I don't hear a sound, I see tears running down his face as he reads.

CHAPTER EIGHTEEN

"MIKE, I really don't understand you." Trisha's eyes are filling with tears as we discuss our problems for the fiftieth time. "What's the matter?"

It seems everyone is asking that question.

"Nothing's the matter, Trish," I say calmly. "I just want to be left alone."

"You never felt that way before." Trisha's face looks accusing.

"I don't even know if I really feel like that now. I just need a little space."

"People don't want space from their girl friends," she says and now the tears start in earnest. "Perhaps you just don't care anymore."

I wish I could pull her close to me and tell her what she wants to hear—that tomorrow everything will be the way it used to be. But I can't. With each passing day, I feel more sure that a woman, no matter how devoted, will never be able to fill the deep emotional needs within me.

I wish Trisha would stop crying. I try to blot her tears with my bandana but she cries harder. I let her cry into my shoulder. I really want to tell her that she should start to see other people, but I know this is not the time to be telling her that. We walk a little while and gradually she quiets down. "Mike, I'm going to go home," she says. "I have to think."

Then she's gone and I stand alone, looking and feeling very helpless.

The next morning I'm confronted by Foxie. He looks at me with a look I've never seen before. "Mike, I'd like to talk to you in my room after school."

I wonder what I've done. Foxie never talks to anyone, unless it's to bawl them out. I really tried hard on my term paper. It can't be that.

The day drags by. At lunchtime I tell Todd that Foxie wants to see me and he makes a funny face.

"What did you do lately?"

I shrug my shoulders. As far as I know, I haven't done anything.

It is with great trepidation that I walk the long tiled hall to Foxie's classroom after school. My feet seem to want to catch on the floors and my palms are sweaty.

I open the door slowly and he's at his desk across the room. He looks over his glasses and says, "Sit down, Mike. I'll be with you in a moment."

I sit down and squirm. I look at the clock and try to keep my mind off what he wants. Perhaps I'm failing his class. Who knows?

He ruffles the papers on his desk and pulls out a file folder. He gestures for me to move closer and I walk stiffly to his side. "Pull up a chair, Mike," he says as he takes his glasses off and looks at me with level gray eyes. On the bridge of his nose are two little indentations from his glasses. His eyebrows are thick and unruly. He almost has the look of a mad genius—someone who might creep around the backstage of an opera and kill people. But when I look closer, I notice that his eyes are kind.

"I suppose you wonder why old Foxie called you in here," he begins.

I smile. He's not so dumb after all. He knows we call him Foxie. "Mike, I found something that gave me some insight into you, and I want to discuss it with you."

He leafs through my term paper and pulls out a sheet of yellow paper. He holds it out to me. The room swims in front of my eyes. It's one of the pieces I've written in my confusion and frustration. One of the papers that says, without a word of a doubt, that I am gay.

My eyes burn and my throat feels like I have a tennis ball in it. Maybe I can deny I wrote it. Perhaps he'll believe me. His eyes grow kinder and he pats the top of my hand. "I just wanted to talk with you about this, Mike. It isn't the end of the world."

I can't believe he's saying that to me.

"So many young people have their lives disrupted by things like this," he continues, "and it isn't fair. Society has decided that on some issues they are to be the judge, the jury, the executioner. Homosexuality is one of those issues. More ignorance surrounds it than almost any other topic. If the true facts were known, perhaps more people would be tolerant, able to understand. But as it is, most people have closed minds on the subject. And that's terrible, because by doing that, they isolate a whole segment of the population that has a lot to offer."

He pulls out a thin, tan book. "This book lists some of the greatest achievers of our world: Michaelangelo, the best painter of all time; Stephen Foster, a songwriter who influenced America; and more recently, Dave Kopay, a professional football player. All homosexual."

He pauses a moment. "Mike, do you understand why I'm taking the time to talk to you?"

I'm almost numbed into silence. To think that Foxie read one of the most personal things about me has my mind spinning. Then on top of that he tries to make me feel good about it. For three years I have made fun of this man behind his back. I have never liked him. At this moment, I have more respect for him than for any other man I have ever known. Because he cares. Because he wants me to know it's all right and that he understands. And because he is taking the time to reach out to another human being when he doesn't have to.

"I really appreciate it." What I really want to do is hug him and tell him he's making my life a lot better.

"I realize you are probably uptight because I read this, but you don't have to be. I will never tell anyone about it, nor will I pretend it's something we shared intentionally. It was by accident that it happened. I'm glad because it's given me a chance to know you better."

"I am uptight. I think I'm the only person in school with these feelings."

"I'm sure you aren't. Kinsey says 10 percent of all males are homosexual. So that means in a school population of 1200 males, about 120 of them are gay."

I grin. "I want to know the other 119." Foxie laughs and I laugh and the tension is gone.

"Do your parents know?" he asks me.

For an instant I panic. Perhaps he will tell them. Then rational thought takes over. He's promised me he will never tell anyone, and I believe him.

"No, they don't. Perhaps I'll tell them someday,

but not yet. I'm afraid of the way they'll react. I know it will be a shock to them."

"Perhaps not." Foxie's gray eyes grow soft. "Parents often know a lot more than we give them credit for."

"My brother Steve is uptight about gays. I'm afraid that he'll hate me."

Foxie says the same thing that Carole did. "Initially he might react strongly, but if he loves you, then he'll come to realize that you're the same person you were before you told him."

"I worry that I'll become like the stereotypical gays. Why does that happen?"

"Do you mean the idea that all gays want to be women, and lisp, and wear dresses?" he asks, and I nod my head numbly. "Well, that's partly because so much secrecy has always surrounded homosexuality. Across America there are millions of gay men living life to the fullest, never lisping or wearing a dress. But they aren't the visible ones. Being gay doesn't make you any less of a man. It just makes you a man with different sexual tastes than other men."

Foxie is a great guy. For a moment I'm tempted to ask how come he knows so much about the subject, but I hesitate. I wonder, for an instant, if he himself is gay. He seems to have a handle on the whole subject. I find myself telling him about Todd and Trisha and the whole mess that my life is in. He listens. It starts to grow dark outside and he switches on the lights in the classroom.

"Thanks so much for hearing me out," I tell him. "I feel like I have so much to say and no one to say it to."

"I'm glad you find me easy to talk to," he says. "I know most of the kids think I'm an old hard-nose. But inside I'm really soft. I'm only strict because I want what's best for all of you. I want you to walk away from my classes with a zest for learning and a way of knowing how to work. College isn't easy, you know."

I agree with him. I'm sure that in the months to come, I'll be his biggest booster.

"Do you think I should tell my dad?"

"You'll know when the time is right," he says, "but meanwhile you have to attend to your life problems. The idea of telling Todd is a good one. You've set a time schedule, and knowing the kind of person you are I'm sure nothing will deter you from it. Once Todd knows and your parents know, you'll have set yourself free. Everyone who loves you now will still love you. If they don't, then they never really loved you anyway. Not in any real way."

We are both exhausted and he asks me to come and talk with him again. He gives me the phone number of a gay hot line in case I feel pressures building and need someone to talk to. He also gives me his home number. We walk down the long tile hallway and our shoes make little slapping noises on the floor, echoing in the empty school.

I don't know how I summon up the courage, but I finally have to ask. "How do you know so much about this? Are you gay?"

He smiles at me, a smile that is filled with about as much wisdom as any one man deserves. "No, Mike, I've been happily married for twenty-five years. But my oldest son, Gary, is gay."

"He's a lucky guy. He has you to talk to."

Pain crosses Foxie's face and the lines appear to deepen as he speaks. "He never gave me that chance. He assumed we wouldn't understand and would hate him, so he left home and we don't know where he is. My talking to you is somehow making up to Gary.

I can't help him now, but if I can help you, Mike, I'll be here when you need me."

We reach the door and go in different directions. "'Night, Mike." He waves his hand at me.

"Good night, Foxie—I mean, good night, sir."

CHAPTER NINETEEN

THE TIME has come to do something about Trisha. I can no longer keep up the act. With this in mind, I ask her to meet me at the malt shop.

She arrives, a little breathless, her face reddened from the cold evening air. She's puzzled because it's the middle of the week and we usually only meet this way on weekends. But this is something I have to do before I go crazy.

I hold her hand at first and she acts a little anxious. She has known for quite some time that something's wrong between us.

"Trisha, we have to talk," I begin, but she cuts me short.

Her blue eyes are welling with tears. "Maybe I don't want to talk."

I try to be gentle. "You know as well as I do that we have to."

"Not here," she says, so we both stand up quietly and walk along the brook path. So much of each of us is tied up in the other. We've seen each other grow and start to develop. We've made love. Why do I feel as if this silent girl beside me is a stranger?

"Mike," she says, with an urgency in her voice, "I don't think I'm ready for this."

"Trish." I suddenly feel a tremendous tenderness for her. "We really have to work this out."

We sit on a tree that has fallen. Both of us are uneasy.

"Who is it, Mike?" she asks. The moon shows that two silver tears have made their way down her face. "Who are you in love with?" The words rush out in a torrent. "I've tried to understand, to give you the space you need. I've talked to lots of my girl friends and they say you aren't seeing anyone else. What is it then? Why do you hate me?" Now she is crying in earnest.

"Trisha, I don't hate you." I hold her close to me and let her cry. "But there's so much going on in my mind right now that I can't resolve. It has nothing at all to do with you. Please believe that."

She isn't buying what I have to say. "Am I too pushy? Or too quiet? Or not good enough in bed? Or frigid? Or ugly?" She is getting louder and louder and sounds almost hysterical.

"Trish, I've told you it has nothing to do with you. It has to do with me."

"Where did I go wrong?" She won't give up. "Sometimes you make it easy for me to hate you, Mike. You're so selfish. You think about yourself so much. What about me?"

It's her plaintive cry "What about me?" that rings in my ears. I want to say "Trisha, don't you understand? I am doing this for you. I'm setting you free to have a full life for yourself. One that I will never be able to give you." But I say, "Trisha, I'm not being selfish, I'm being fair."

"You think it's fair to hurt me like this?" She is

really crying now and I helplessly dab at her face with my handkerchief.

"Trish, I don't want to hurt you. You're one of the special people in my life."

"I'm not even as special as Todd is." She is striking out now, unloading all of the hostility that has built up over the past few months. "You'd rather spend time with him."

Suddenly she stops and her eyes narrow. "You're probably a fairy."

I feel as if she's kicked me or given me a good punch in the stomach.

"You say there's no other girl," she rages at me. "Well, then, what is it, Mike?"

"I don't know." My head is hanging. I don't know how to fight her anymore. She has come too close to the truth.

She opens her purse and takes out a package and throws it at me. "Here, Mike, you can have it all back," she yells. "Everything you ever gave me. I never want to see you again."

She runs through the woods and I can't catch up to her. I hear her sobs as she runs. After she's gone, I stand still for a long while with tears running down my face. I have really hurt her. I never started out to do that. I thought perhaps we could reach an agreement that both of us could live with. I guess I don't understand girls. Perhaps I should have leveled with Trisha as soon as I knew what my feelings were, but it's been so hard just dealing with me. I have been selfish, though, holding on to her like a child holds on to a security blanket.

The next day in school the repercussions start to hit me. Her girl friends snub me. One chubby girl named Michelle says, "Mike, you have some nerve, hurting Trisha like that."

What in God's name has she told them? I try to

talk to her at lunchtime but she gives me a look that can best be described as evil.

"Let me alone, Mike, before I dump this plate on you."

I back away—she has spaghetti on her plate.

"What happened?" Todd asks me. "Everyone is saying you did a number on Trisha."

"Todd, have I ever been really mean?"

"Not to me, but then we've never been involved romantically." He laughs.

She sends me a note during gym. It's delivered by a guy in my class who gives me a funny look. "Trisha says you might be a queer," he says snidely. Then he laughs. "Girls always get impossible when you break up with them."

Even Dee asks me what happened. She and Trisha have never been close but now even she is taking Trisha's side. "Boys can be mean," she says. "Oh, I know you don't want to be mean, but it comes across that way."

When I finally get a minute alone, I open the note. The handwriting tells me Trish is under great duress. She is writing what she can't say: *I guess I'm so hurt that I want to hurt you. I have to do it.* The note isn't even signed. I crumple it into a ball and throw it away. I can't let all of this get to me any more than it already has.

CHAPTER TWENTY

"MIKE, what's a jet plane do to stay up in the air?" Jeffie is sitting at the foot of my bed as I do homework. Every few minutes he asks me some dumb question to make me pay attention to him.

"I have no idea. I guess it's the motors."

"But if it's heavy, why doesn't it fall down?"

He smiles at me and I have to smile back. His one big tooth is starting to grow in and his face looks older to me.

"Mike, why don't you want to talk?" The question hangs in the air.

"I have homework to do," I say. Then I pause a minute. Mom is at a meeting. Steve, as usual, is reading. Dad is watching television. Jeffie is lonely.

So I put my book down. "Want to play a game of Go Fish or War?" The small face brightens. "Sure, Mike. I'll get the cards."

Sometimes I forget he's only six. I expect him to

realize that sometimes I don't have time for him. But tonight he appeals to a soft spot and I relent.

I think of Foxie and of our talk. He made time for me; I can do as much for my little brother.

When I was six, I was different from Jeffie. My world was far smaller than his. Steve and I had each other to play with and I was content to stay in my child's world. That's not the case with Jeff. He wants to be everywhere, to touch everything, to sense the world. Maybe he's better off than Steve and I were.

He comes back with the cards jammed between his hands, half spilling them on to the floor as he walks. "Are you Trisha's boyfriend anymore?" he asks.

"We're taking a breather from each other." I try to explain the logistics of breaking up to Jeffie and he just frowns, a crease wrinkling his forehead. "Boy, Steve let Carole get away. Now you let Trisha get away. Christopher Michael already has a baby niece. I'm never gonna get one, am I?"

Christopher Michael is Jeffie's best friend. He's smaller than Jeffie and a lot quieter. He always lets Jeff be the leader. In many ways they remind me of Todd and me. I hope they stay friends as long as we have. It's very important to have a good friend.

"Christopher Michael's just lucky, I guess."

He jumps on me, scattering the cards to the floor. "Come on, Mike, get married, will ya?"

I am overcome with feelings of tenderness for my little brother, and I give him a long, hard hug. He squirms from my grasp and demands equal nieces with Christopher Michael. "The baby drinks a bottle and Christopher Michael gets to feed her and burp her."

It all sounds ominous to me. "Does he get to change the dirty diapers too?"

Todd arrives at this time and plops on my bed. He wrestles with Jeff for a few moments, then the three of us engage in a hard and fast game of war. Todd wins and Jeffie says he's a cheater.

"You dealed them," he says, "and you dealed yourself all the aces."

His loss has taken away his interest in cards. He gives us a mock bow and exits.

"Jeffie is getting so tall," Todd says. "He was such a munchkin for so long—I was worried he'd never grow." Then he smiles and wrinkles his nose. "But then you were always such a squirt too, until you were fourteen."

Todd was always taller than me. We used to measure every week to see who was bigger, and for years Todd won. Then I started to grow, and within a few weeks I was taller. Todd never caught up. I'm sure the same will be true for Jeffie.

"I was really mad when you started to get taller," Todd admits in a moment of weakness, "but I guess I'll get over it someday."

We decide to go to the beach to run. It's the first nice day we've had this year and Todd says it's a shame to waste it.

"The beach is always great on the first good day," he says. Both of us, I'm sure, are mentally recounting the endless times we've run on the beach.

I'm glad I grew up on the beach. It's almost a part of me. I don't think I'd be happy living where I could never see the ocean.

We drive to the beach and strip down to sweatshirts and shorts. The wind makes the hair on my legs bristle and goose bumps start to appear. Then we start to run, and within minutes I'm dripping with sweat.

Todd is actually a better runner than I am. I'm taller and my legs are longer, but Todd has a style of running that sets him apart from others. He's fast and knows how to keep a pace.

Todd is so well coordinated—he's almost like a

song in motion. He never tires as easily as I do, either.

After we run to the rock jetty we sit and watch the sea gulls. They are amazing creatures, graceful and always beautiful.

"How are things with you and Dee?"

"They're fine." He smiles at me. "I know you've been having problems with Trish but they'll pass. Problems always do."

"I think if we were married the problems would be called irreconcilable differences," I say.

Todd laughs. "Yeah, that's what I had with Marcy."

He and Dee have managed to keep their relationship intact for many reasons—mostly because they care so much about each other and both are willing to give as much as they get. That has to be the basis for any relationship. They finally did make love, but Todd says it was different from what he had imagined.

"I guess I'm more mature or something," he'd confided, "but with Dee the lovemaking is just that—making love. We're gonna get married, ya know, as soon as we graduate."

I feel a lump in my throat. Then I'll lose him for sure. We are so close this day. After the tide starts to come in, we both lie on the sand, our faces to the winter sun, and we talk and laugh and share secrets the way we always have done. But inside I feel a deep sense of loss. I know that now we are almost grown, and with that growing we are gaining but also losing. Our lives are already beginning to take separate paths. Someday Todd will be gone. And so will I.

He is unaware of the way I am watching him. I admire the way his blond hair falls onto his brow, the curve of his eyebrows, the way his dark eyelashes curve upward, the set to his chin. The sun makes his hair seem like a halo and when he raises his eyes to look at me, I see all of the tranquillity and peace of the sea in them.

I want to hold him close to me. The feeling is overpowering. So I stand up and shout, "Let's race."

"No fair, Mike," he screams after me. "You have yourself a head start."

I run until the emotions of the moment subside.

For once, I'm way ahead of Todd. I figure that's because he isn't running away from anything the way I am.

When he finally catches up with me, he tousles my hair. "Mike, you oughta be a sprinter."

"Maybe next year," I say.

When we get home there's an envelope waiting for me. Mom looks at it suspiciously. Even Todd wants to know what's inside. I did send for some material about homosexuality, so I take the envelope and toss it on my desk. "I'll look at it later," I say offhandedly, and pray that no one makes a move for the envelope.

I'm lucky. They don't. As soon as Todd leaves, I tear the envelope open. Sure enough, it's the literature I sent for. I pore over it eagerly. On the bottom of one pamphlet there's a phone number that says, "For more information call..." I file the number away in my address book under the name of *Jan.* No one will ever guess what it really is.

The pamphlets are informative, but some of them are hard to understand. I guess my experience is pretty limited as far as being gay goes.

Steve comes in while I'm reading. "Why are you reading that?" His voice is surprised. He takes the pamphlet from my hand.

"I'm doing a report for school."

He laughs. "Things sure have changed in four years," he says. "We didn't ever discuss that stuff when I was in school."

"I think gays are persecuted," I say.

"Don't get carried away, Mike. Every minority is

persecuted. Perhaps there's a reason. Would you just consider that once before you get on your soapbox?"

"Like what?" I say, eager to display my newfound knowledge.

"Gays molest little boys." He stands, hands on hips, looking smug.

I can be smug, too. "That isn't true. Most children are molested by straight men."

"Who told you that?" Steve looks upset.

I pull out the pamphlet called *Most Asked Questions about Gay Life-styles* and show it to him. There it is. Question fourteen. "No, it isn't true that gays molest little boys. In fact, studies done by the U.S. Government show that when children are molested it is most often by heterosexual men."

Steve hands me back the pamphlet. "It's propaganda put out by gay activists," he says.

"This is put out by the United States Department of Health," I argue, but Steve doesn't want to listen to me.

"You're just like Carole," he says. "Both of you are dumb on certain subjects."

I put my hands on my hips and stare him down. "Maybe Carole was right leaving you. Maybe her new boyfriend is more sensitive."

He smiles at me, a smile that really isn't a smile. "Sometimes I think you were dropped on your head when you were a kid."

"Sometimes I think you were hatched."

Steve is the one person who really bothers me. Because we are brothers, because we've shared so much for so long, I want to share this with him. But I can't. Steve would never understand it.

After Steve goes to bed, I dial the number for the gay hot line. For an hour and a half, I sit and talk to a kind anonymous voice. I'm curled up on a hard dining room chair, pouring my heart out. The voice reassures me, comforts me, tells me that talking it out is the only way to resolve it. He asks if my parents know yet and I try to explain the whole situation. Then I start to talk about Steve. Before I'm finished the tears are running down my face. "I want him to love me and to accept me," I sob. "We've always been so close."

"There are no guarantees," the guy says. "We can only do what we can do. The most important thing is to know yourself first, then everything else will fall into place."

He tells me to call back if I need to talk. I'm sure I'll be calling back—I need someone to help me through this. He gives me the number of a church-oriented gay group called Dignity. Perhaps I'll call them and attend a meeting. Maybe they have some of the elusive answers.

CHAPTER TWENTY-ONE

I SQUIRM in my chair and look at the mimeographed paper in my hands. It says, "God doesn't make junk." And since God made gays, they aren't junk either. I guess that's the premise of this meeting. I was so careful driving here. I told Todd I was dating a girl from out of town and I told my parents the same thing. I look around the assembled group. None of the people look any different from me. Some are older, some are women. But we all share the same problems. We're all dealing with being gay.

One guy about my age is there with his mother. She seems totally supportive of him. Before the meeting she tells me there is a group for parents of gays. I tell her my parents don't know and she smiles at me and pats my hand. "Tell them soon, Mike."

Everyone is caring in this group. Although I am new, each of them speaks to me. The priest who runs the group takes me aside and tells me he's glad I've come.

The discussion this evening is "Being gay in the

1980s." The topics focus on the repeal of gay rights in some states and the effect the new moral tone of the nation is going to have on homosexuals.

"Part of the reason we are discriminated against is because so few people really understand homosexuality," says one man. "When I was young no one ever mentioned it. Now it's more visible, but we as a group have to do something to promote a more positive image of gay people."

"Misconceptions are the usual thing," a boy my age says. "Everyone has a mental picture of a gay person that isn't true."

He's right. I think of Coach Wheeler and the soccer team. To them, gay is synonymous with degeneracy.

"How do you feel about being gay, Mike?" the priest asks.

I try to shrink into my chair. "I don't really know yet, except that I'm scared and I worry a lot about people finding out."

"How old are you?" he asks.

"I'm seventeen on my next birthday, and I've known for about a year. This past year has been the hardest of my life."

"I want you to know that we understand, and that we're here to help you through all of this."

Then the discussion turns to gay political clout. I can't deal with these issues yet. I'm too busy trying to find out who I am and where I'm coming from. Politics are too far out of reach for me so far.

I still want to know the basic things, like how being gay will affect my whole life. That's far more relevant to me than the political clout I'll have.

After the official part of the meeting is over, everyone socializes. For me, this is the best part. It's a chance to talk to other gay people and find out how they deal with all of these things.

"How did you tell your mother?" I ask Darren, the guy my age.

He says it wasn't easy. "I thought she'd hate me. I was sure she'd throw me out of the house. But I had to tell her because I was going crazy."

"And she understood?" I ask Darren.

He smiles. "She's here, isn't she?"

He says his father wasn't so understanding but that he's trying. "They belong to Parents of Gays," he says. "They find it helps them a lot."

I wish Mom and Dad knew so they could join. I think that in my case, Dad will accept it easier than Mom.

"My brother is very anti-gay," I tell Darren.

"So is my brother," Darren says, "and it hurts me a lot. But I only hope that someday he'll change his views. I can't change mine if I want to."

I think in one sentence Darren has summed it all up. "I can't change mine if I want to."

God knows if I could I would have changed mine. It would be so much easier for me and for everyone else involved. I could still be dating Trisha and still be Todd's good friend and look forward to a home and family. But it isn't that simple. For me, things have to be this way.

I'm glad I came to this meeting. I can see it will make me feel even better about myself, stronger somehow. I feel especially happy when the door opens and Foxie walks in.

Foxie has been great. His son was a jerk not to confide in him. When Trisha and I broke up I needed someone to reassure me and Foxie was right there. Todd teases me about liking Foxie. He doesn't understand. How can I expect him to?

"How was the meeting Mike?" Foxie asks. I tell him it was fine.

"I wish I was twenty-six and all of this was past history," I say.

Foxie smiles. "Don't wish your life away. It will pass fast enough."

I'm sure he's right. These days I'm obsessed with calendars. It's only three months—a little less—until I tell Todd. I've rehearsed what to say a hundred times. I haven't found the exact words yet, but by July Fourth, I'll have them down pat.

I fantasize a lot about Todd. I think everyone has fantasies and for some people they provide an outlet that wouldn't otherwise be there. I think that's the way it is with my fantasies about Todd.

But I'm wise enough to know that my fantasies are just dreams and not reality. Todd will never be able to love me the way I love him and I can't ever ask him to. That's the reality. In my fantasies he loves me as much as I love him. We take long walks on sunlit beaches and we kiss and hold hands and share everything. The only person I've dared to share these feelings with is Foxie. He doesn't laugh at them. He just listens. That's all I need right now.

The group makes me feel better about myself. It seems all of the experiences of these past few months are giving me a more positive self-image. It seems funny that a few months ago I thought I was alone in this. I think that's the most frightening thing of all—to feel isolation and loneliness. To feel different, less than others.

Now I know I'm the same person I always was. But to try to express that to someone else is next to impossible. Especially my peer group. If they hear the word *gay,* they close their minds like steel traps. There is no reasoning with them, no point of discussion. I now also realize I won't always be a teenager. As I grow my problems will change—for the better in some cases, for the worse in others. But my peer group will change too. Half of them will become more tolerant, the other half will be happy to see me tarred and feathered. If I could have one wish, it would be for every straight person in the world to live one week as a gay person. Perhaps then they would be able to see that we are not really so different—we are the same.

Maybe I will choose a career that will help the gay community—especially young gays who are just coming out. I've decided to become a counselor—a person people can talk to and be comfortable with. My own experience will help me in this field, I'm sure.

Sometimes, I feel like two different people—Mike Ramsey, devoted son, good student, soccer player, trustworthy friend—and Mike Ramsey, introverted, panic-stricken, and fearful. On some days number one is the person I am, and on other days number two makes me want to jump into the ocean and never come out.

But more and more the two me's are coming closer together. The fears are starting to be quelled, my introversion has given me insight into myself, and the panic is now sporadic. I know I've grown in every area.

My thoughts are interrupted when Foxie asks, "How do you feel about stopping for a cup of coffee on the way home?" I agree it's a good idea and after saying good-bye to a few friends we leave the meeting.

Over coffee we discuss the upcoming baseball season, the style of girls' dresses for the prom, and the economy. Neither of us mentions the gay issue. Sometimes even I need a break from it.

When I get home I find Todd asleep in my bed. I try to be as quiet as I can but he sits up and smiles at me. "Tell me all about her. I want to know all of the details."

I sit on the bed and start to weave a fantasy: "Well, she's about five-four," I begin. "Her name is Laurie and she lives in Asbury Park. She likes to disco and she has a pet dog named Rags."

I think I should win some sort of award for fast

ad-libbing. I'd almost forgotten that I was supposed to be out on a date tonight.

"Is she built?" Todd has a way of breaking through to the nitty-gritty.

"Not really. She's thin." Can't make her perfect, can I?

"How thin?" Todd is getting more interested.

"Not that thin, but thin." I try to sound convincing.

"What color hair? Eyes? More details, man." Todd is being a pain in the neck.

"Blond, blue, and she wears size seven shoes."

My sarcasm is lost on Todd: "How do you know her shoe size? I don't even know Dee's."

"I get all the facts."

"Let's double-date," he says, and I agree to discuss that possibility with Laurie.

"Can I stay overnight?"

"It looks like you already are."

He moves over in the narrow bed. "Here, I'm not that fat, you can sleep here too."

I look at the bed for a long moment. I debate what to do. Since we were six, we've slept together in this bed. But now we're both almost six feet tall and the bed is very small. I don't know if it's a good idea. I never want Todd to suspect until I tell him on July Fourth.

I make a bed on the floor with extra blankets and Todd gives me a lopsided grin. "Boy, you make me feel like I have body odor."

"No, but you have other things," I joke, and he hits me with a pillow.

It's like a signal. Both of us laugh and thrash each other with pillows until the feathers are flying through the air. Todd has some stuck in his hair and he looks so funny I start to laugh. Jeffie appears suddenly, a rumpled little figure holding a teddy bear in one arm. He surveys the wreckage of the room. Feathers are floating everywhere, and some land in his hair and on his outstretched hand. He rubs his eyes.

"Steve's gonna be mad when he sees this room," he says. "Can I play too?"

He drops his teddy bear and springs to life. The three of us hit each other with pillows until we all collapse with laughter.

"Someday when we're older Christopher and I will have as much fun as you guys do, won't we?" Jeffie asks us.

"I'm sure you already have fun," Todd assures him.

"But we'll have girls and cars and be able to smoke and have beers." Jeffie lets us know in one sentence what he thinks of us.

"You'll be a lady-killer," Todd tells him, "if only you can get your hair to lie flat and if your teeth ever grow in."

"They'll grow in." Jeffie is sure of this. "See?" He shows a mouth full of gaps and teeth half-grown.

"Then you'll be a lady-killer," Todd teases. "Just like Jack the Ripper."

Jeffie starts to hit Todd with his teddy bear and the stuffing starts to come out. Teddy is Jeffie's bed companion and when he sees the rip in the bear, he starts to sob. "Oh look, teddy's sick."

Todd kneels beside him, all the frivolity of the moment before forgotten. "We'll give him stitches, just like you got when you cut your foot," Todd tells him. Then he gets the sewing kit and stitches up the bear as good as new.

"Get me a bandage," he tells Jeffie, and my little brother brings him a roll of gauze. Todd bandages the sewn part, then hands the bear to Jeffie.

"Bring him back in a week, sir, and we'll remove the bandage. He'll be as good as new."

Jeffie hugs Todd in a bear hug. "Thanks so much. You saved teddy's life."

I watch the scene, loving both of them so much.

CHAPTER TWENTY-TWO

IT'S A bright sunny day and I've pledged myself to spend it with Jeffie. June is such a beautiful month at the Jersey shore. The water is a beautiful green color and the sun is warm and good for tanning.

And, as Jeffie says, "The beach is just lying there waiting for me to dig it up." We both get an added bonus when Dad says he wants to go along with us.

The drive to the beach takes only minutes, and we have the whole place to ourselves. The sea grass is still very green—the sun hasn't bleached it out yet. Sea gulls swarm overhead in hopes that the bag Jeffie carries contains some stale bread for them.

Dad smiles. "I remember when you and Steve were smaller and a trip to the beach meant carrying tubes, blankets, a cooler of cold drinks, Handi-Wipes, three towels, two shovels and pails, and a rubber surfboard. At least we've trained Jeffie to pack and carry his own gear. It gives me a rest."

We spread the blanket on the sand and Jeffie heads

for the edge of the water. The ocean is still freezing and it will remain so until the end of August. But Jeffie only plays with the waves anyway. If he does go in, the sight of an oncoming wave is enough to send him scurrying back to shore. Someday he'll get knocked over and then he'll learn to respect the ocean. It happened to both Steve and me. I'm sure it will happen to Jeffie too.

Jeffie unearths his shovel and starts to dig. I fall asleep, lulled by the gentle slapping of waves and the hot sun on my face. I always get the best tan in the family. My skin tone is a little darker than the others, and it only takes a little sun to make me brown.

"Hey, Mike, bury me!" The small voice is insistent. I open my eyes to see Jeffie's face peering into mine.

"Sure, Jeff," I say, sitting up. My legs are already starting to turn brown. I stretch and turn and feel the way the sun makes my body tingle.

Jeffie's nose is getting red, so I coat it with zinc oxide. He looks like a little monster from the deep, with his red nose and bright white face. We dig a hole together and I bury him. I've always hated the feeling of sand on me, but Jeffie loves it.

Dad looks up from the book he's reading and says he wishes he'd brought along a camera. "I'd like to be able to capture these times," he says. "Soon you'll be away at college and they won't happen anymore."

Even Jeffie, up to his chin in sand, grows subdued. "I need a new brother, Daddy."

"Mike will still be your brother," Dad says. "He'll just be in college."

Jeffie looks like he's going to cry. I wish I could take him with me. We play in the sand for a few more hours until Jeffie falls asleep on the edge of the blanket, his thumb in his mouth, his head resting on his rubber tube.

"Isn't he cute?" Dad asks. "I wish I had three more kids to raise."

"Aren't you glad we're finally growing up?" I ask. "You can have some time for yourself."

"I don't want time for myself. You and your brothers are my life. The reason I've worked so hard."

He thinks a minute and his blue eyes grow misty. "When the job is two-thirds over you get upset. You wish it could still be under way in full force."

I feel sad. Dad is upset because this year I'll be a senior. "I'll still be here another year, and you still have Jeffie."

"Mike, for some reason, you've always been the one I'm closest to," Dad confides. "Don't tell your brothers, but I always felt you were mine, while Steve and Jeffie are Mom's. I can't explain it. From the time you were a baby, you were instinctively closer to me. You were never as happy when Mom held you. If you were hurt you ran to me. I guess because you favored me, I favored you. It will be very hard for me to let go. To see you as a man, instead of as a little boy who needs me to watch out for him."

I want to hug my dad. He always makes me feel so special. Perhaps he senses I'm the one who needs him the most.

"I hope I can live up to your expectations, Dad. I never want to let you down."

"Just be a good person. That's all anyone can ask. Be fair and just in your dealings in this old world. If you are, then Mom and I have done a good job in raising you."

I worry a lot that the fact that I'm gay will disappoint Dad. I long to ask him if it will make any difference. But I look at my little brother, then look at Dad, and decide the time isn't quite right yet. I want Todd to know first.

"How is Jeff Hart?" I ask Dad.

Dad smiles. "He's off having a fling in San Francisco. Sometimes I think he'll never be ready to settle down."

"Isn't that true of most gay people?" I ask, opening the subject up again.

"I don't know," Dad says. "In my experience most gays don't settle down because there is so much pressure on their relationships from society. They can never be in the open, and anything that has to be surrounded with secrecy has trouble surviving."

"The world can be a stupid place sometimes, can't it?"

He nods. "In the case of gay people, it's very stupid," he agrees.

I'm glad my dad is the kind of man that he is. He isn't the type to make judgments and for that reason alone, I think I'm one of the luckiest guys around. Lots of my friends have parents who are so against everything that they aren't for anything. That's not the way with my parents at all. In the long run this may be what saves me.

Lying on the beach with my dad and Jeffie, the whole scheme of things seems to fit. It isn't always this way. There are times when it all has me puzzled and bewildered. But lying here, with Dad next to me, I feel protected. Just like in the old days, when I counted on him to care for me. I know in my heart if I told Dad right now that I was gay, he'd still love me. Perhaps he'd even love me more. But somehow I'm not ready to tell him yet.

"Is there anything any of us could do to make you not love us?" I ask.

Dad smiles. "Nope. There's nothing that awful. I loved you the minute I saw you lying in that little basket in the hospital and I've loved you ever since. It's a love that's grown as the years have passed. You and your brothers are too good for me to ever stop loving you. I think you're the best parts of Mom and me. So I'll never stop loving you, no matter what."

I feel like I should say amen, but instead I turn my attention to Jeffie. I pinch his small toe. His feet are so square. And his toes look manicured. On the big toe someone—likely Mom—has painted the nail with red polish. On one ankle he wears his perpetual bandage. His knees are scraped and his bathing suit is too big. I envy Jeffie. I wish I was six and sleeping on my tube with Dad nearby to love and protect me. He has so many more years of that role. I say a silent prayer that Jeffie will never have to face what I've faced this year. I'd do anything to spare him that.

Finally Jeffie wakens and he digs into his little knapsack for stale bread. The gulls swoop down and take the bread from his outstretched hands. They are gentle, never making too aggressive a move, never frightening Jeffie.

"I love you," he shouts to them as he races down the beach, a trail of them flying after him. "I love you all so much."

Jeffie loves everyone and everything. That's a tribute to Mom and Dad.

"Well, guys," Dad says. "Think it's time to take a walk?"

Jeffie grabs his hand and pulls Dad after him. He picks up all kinds of sea objects as we walk—the hollow shell of a crab long dead, some seashells that are broken and chipped, some seaweed.

"Tell me who lives in here," Jeffie demands, and Dad kneels down beside him.

I have a flashback that is as vivid as the day it happened. We are walking along this same beach. Steve is running ahead of us and I am as little as Jeffie is now. I spot a shell. "Daddy," I demand, "tell me who lived in here."

And then, just as he does now with Jeffie, he knelt down beside me and drew my sandy little body close to his own. "An old lady clam lived in here," he told me. "But she was always mean to the other sea animals, so they evicted her. Her house is empty now and will stay that way until she mends her ways and can live in peace with others."

I always thought the story was true until I was much older, but Jeffie isn't so easily fooled. He hangs his head a moment, then looks at Dad with his fingers hanging in one corner of his mouth.

"You made that up," he accuses. "Look at all these empty shells. Are all old lady clams bad?" He races along the beach and returns with an armful of clams. "Were they all bad?"

Dad laughs and tousles Jeffie's hair "See, Mike? That's what I mean. You and I are the dreamers in this family. Jeffie isn't one of us. He knows the facts and he deals with them. You and I always look for something more."

Then Dad takes Jeffie's hand and puts his arm around my shoulder and we walk back to the blanket. It's been the nicest day I've had in a long time.

We sit for a while longer, then Dad says perhaps it's time we went home. "Mom will be wondering where we are," he says. "She'll think we've been kidnapped by a band of beach bums." I hate to see the day end. The sun is low in the sky and it's a bright flaming orange. Tomorrow will be as hot as today. Soon the tourists will come and we'll have to surrender the beaches until fall.

We ride home and sing an old song that Dad likes. It's fun to forget all my problems and just be a kid again.

When we pull up to the house Todd and Dee are on the porch waiting. Those two are almost inseparable. But when we get closer I see tears on Dee's face.

"What's the matter?" I ask, for Todd looks sober, too.

"My aunt and uncle are sending me to Europe for

the summer," Dee says. The tears start again. "Isn't that awful?"

I look at Todd and know that I miss all of the time we used to spend together before Dee.

"Really terrible," I say, but I don't mean it at all.

CHAPTER TWENTY-THREE

IT'S THE last day of school and that means general hysteria. In a way it makes me sad. After this there will only be one more school closing for me. All of the kids I've been with for the past twelve years will then be just a memory—I'll be facing all new people and things in college. Perhaps that's when I'll really start to grow.

This year, school closes on my birthday—June 15. I get lots of cards about astrology. Everyone, it seems, is looking into it and really believing what they hear. I am Gemini—the twins. That's appropriate. I am the twins—two separate people.

Foxie calls me into his classroom and tells me to have a good summer. He makes me promise to call if I need anything. I've grown to love and respect this man. When he hands me my report card, he smiles at me. "I love you like a son, Mike, but I still can't give you a better grade than a two. Work harder next year."

I smile at him and we shake hands in a formal man-to-man way; then we forget that and hug each other. "Thanks so much for everything," I tell him, "and have a great summer."

"Good luck on July Fourth," he says. "You'd better call and let me know the outcome of that one."

I've circled July Fourth on the calendar. It will be the start of a whole new life for me.

After school, Mom is acting funny. She keeps sending me out on errands. I suppose she's trying to bake me a cake and wants me out of the way.

I decide to help her, so I stay away for most of the afternoon. I walk to the beach and watch the gulls. Then I go to the hangout and have a soda. I can't find Todd. Likely he and Dee are off someplace crying together. She leaves for Europe in two days. I can't wait.

When I get to my block I see Jeffie on the stoop. As soon as he sees me, he runs inside. I wonder if he's broken something of mine. When he does that he always hides from me. That's how I know he's done something wrong. He hides under the bed. He always chooses the same place to hide. I'll know where to grab him if he has broken something.

I walk inside and everyone yells "Surprise." The table is set with all kinds of cold cuts and a big birthday cake in the center blazes with candles. Todd is there, and so are Trisha and Dee and Roger. Roger and Trisha are dating and I'm glad for both of them. And my brother Steve, and Jeffie, and Mom and Dad—everyone's here.

They all smile at me. "We didn't think you were ever going to come home," they say. Slowly all of the gang show up—most of the soccer team, some of the cheerleaders, and Coach Wheeler. My parents aren't aware of Foxie or I'm sure they would have invited him.

I put on my best party face and spend a lot of time

talking to everyone. After all, I'll only be around them for one more year. I have to store up lots of memories.

Todd hands me a package that's wrapped in paper from a comic strip. For years, every gift we give each other is wrapped this way. It goes back to the days when we were small.

I open it and tears come to my eyes. It's an accumulation of every gift we ever gave each other over the years—a shiny silver kaleidoscope—we fought over the one I gave him when we were seven and we broke it. Two bags of marbles—one cat eyes, the other pureys. How we hoarded them. Three packs of bubble gum with baseball cards inside—we both had a stack of them in our back pockets for years. A deck of cards, a packet of magic tricks... God, how can I ever forget Todd? Our lives are intertwined so closely that we'll never be free from each other.

Even Dad smiles at the gifts. "Remember when the two of you were doing all the magic shows?" He laughs. "Todd could never quite get the hang of the egg trick and every time he did it, the egg would break in his hands. He'd get so mad. He'd end up throwing all of the eggs on the floor."

Todd never did have much patience.

Dee laughs. She loves the old stories about Todd. The last gift in his parcel is a bag that's carefully wrapped. It has a tie around the top and there's a note attached. It reads, "In case you still want to be blood brothers, I brought the goods." Inside are a dozen very ripe cherries.

Oh God, Todd, what am I going to do if you end up hating me? Somehow, I haven't really been able to face the possibility of what I will do if Todd doesn't understand. More than anything in this world, I want him to say it's okay with him. More than my dad and mom. More than anyone.

Trisha gives me an impersonal gift of a wallet.

It's funny—she seems like a stranger now. I wonder if she's sleeping with Roger? I guess the sad part is that I really don't care if she is. It's hard to believe we were once so close.

Jeffie's painted me a picture. I look at it and admire it, but I can't really tell what it is.

"Explain the artwork, Jeff," Todd says.

Jeffie obliges. "This is me and Mike and Daddy. We're on the beach and we're having a nice day. These are sea gulls"—he points to some splashes of white—"and these are sandpipers. I call it 'A Day at the Beach.' Good name, right, Todd?"

Todd smiles at him. "A darned good name, Jeffie."

Todd always says that someday the world will hear about Jeffie. I hope he's right. Trisha always said Todd was right—that in later life Jeff would likely be someone famous. Everyone seems to think he's preordained for something special. I hope they're right.

Coach Wheeler's gift is a book on soccer technique. "It's good to learn from the pros, Mike," he says. "We can't ever know enough."

The candles are blown out and Mom sniffles a little. "Oh, Mike, you're getting so grown-up. Now if only you'd learn to clean your room."

Even on my birthday she nags.

My parents have a special gift for me. Dad covers my eyes as Mom brings the package. It's small and square and well wrapped. There's a red bow on it. I open it slowly and to my delight I find a set of car keys inside. I can't believe it—my own car.

Mom and Dad both hug me, and Dad says, "It's used but it's clean and it runs really well."

Todd sighs. "Tell my dad about this, will ya?"

Birthdays form a collage in my mind. First, I'm so small that Dad has to hoist me up to blow out the candles, then I'm on a level with the cake, then suddenly I have to bend down to blow them out. Each year the parties are crowded with kids I play with and people special to me. The only constant is Todd. If I look at all of the pictures of all of the parties, his face is always there.

For years the highlight of the parties was "Pin the Tail on the Donkey." It was so much fun. First we'd be blindfolded and spun around until we were so dizzy we could hardly stand. Then we'd grope in the darkness to the shrieks of the other kids. At age eleven, it gave way to Post Office. That year Todd kissed eighteen different girls and three days later came down with chicken pox.

He blamed it on me and my party.

After everyone leaves, I help Mom clean up. "Thanks for helping, Mike. And listen, I want to say I'm sorry for always being on your case. I just want you to grow up right."

Jeffie stands at the sink washing the dishes. His sleeves are rolled up and he has an apron tied under his arms. Steve is drying. I'm the only one who doesn't have to work—after all, it's my birthday.

"Can I go for a ride in the new car?" Steve asks. He also got a car when he turned seventeen. Mine is a nice little convertible. Dad says it will be great for commuting to and from college.

After everyone else is asleep I'm still wide awake. I go downstairs and watch the late-night *Mary Tyler Moore* reruns and munch on some potato chips left over from the party. On the living room wall are portraits of Steve and I when we were small. I am missing several teeth and Steve's hair is slicked back and parted. So much has happened since that time.

I hear a noise and turn around to see Steve. "Want some company?"

We sit quietly and talk a little, sharing a moment with each other.

"Mike, I'm sorry I've been such a jerk lately," he

says suddenly. "We've always been so close but this thing with Carole really threw me."

"I know, Steve. You don't have to explain."

"But I do have to explain. I've been a jerk to everyone who matters, it seems."

"That's okay, everyone is entitled sometimes," I say. "But now it's over."

"You're a special kid brother," he says, and I feel as close to him as when he'd carry me to bed with him. "Let's make a pact to never let petty differences come between us," he says.

I laugh. "Should we use Todd's cherries and be blood brothers?"

Steve laughs too. "It's too late. We already are blood brothers."

"Steve, I hope nothing will ever come between us," I say, thinking about the bombshell I will lay on him sometime this summer.

"Look, kid, I'm your brother and you're stuck with me, and that's the way it is."

I hug him and he hugs me back. This has been an evening for closeness. We both go upstairs and we lay in bed and talk for a while, then Steve falls asleep. I feel reassured knowing that everyone really does love me. They all proved that today, didn't they?

Steve's even breathing lulls me to a semiconscious state as I think about what lies ahead. Before summer is over, everyone will know. That's the way it has to be. They'll know and we'll see what happens. But looming ahead—only days away—is July Fourth. I raise my eyes skyward to where God, if he exists, lives. Just in case I say a small prayer: "Please help me cope with all that lies ahead. I'll need your help."

CHAPTER TWENTY-FOUR

JULY FOURTH. Independence Day. A time to celebrate. I waken and have the urge to go back to sleep. This is the day I've planned and waited for for the past six months. It's finally here and I keep waiting for the angel of doom to fly down and be a party to it.

Dee has been gone for two weeks. Todd and I have spent most of the summer thus far together. We camped out a few nights at Mount Laurel, minus Coach Wheeler, and we've spent a lot of time on the beach. Both of us are brown as Indians and Todd's hair is streaked blonder by the sun.

I wish today was over, but it stretches ahead, long and never-ending. It is a day of reckoning. A day for truths to be told. The end of all pretenses. The birth and beginning of a new me. Now to get the courage to do it.

Todd is coming by early and we're spending the day at the beach. I've rehearsed in my mind so many times how to say what is in my heart. But when the moment actually comes, I'm sure I'll freeze up.

I do everything I have to do mechanically. I shower and shave. Then I dress in faded cut-offs and sneakers. I brush my teeth twice, as if by doing that I will have good luck.

I wish I had a rabbit's foot or a magic rock to hold on to. I don't. Mom asks me what the problem is and I give her my widest grin.

"Nothing. Why should anything be the matter?"

"You look like you just lost your best friend," she says.

I think, I just might.

Jeffie begs to go along with us, but I cite crowded holiday conditions as a reason not to take him. "Tomorrow, Jeff." In my mind I say, *After it's all over with. You don't know what's going to happen today and you can't understand it, so please be a good little guy and leave me alone.*

He smiles at me. "Tomorrow, then?" I push his hair back from his eyes and hug him so tight that he squirms to get away.

"Yes, tomorrow."

Christopher Michael comes to the door and asks for Jeffie and the two of them disappear. Mom laughs. "They remind me of you and Todd."

Foxie calls and wishes me luck. "I have a lot of faith in Todd," he says. "If I were you I wouldn't worry too much."

I thank him for calling and promise to call him later on.

I get my things for the beach and pack them into my knapsack. Todd arrives at eleven o'clock and we walk, as we have every summer, up Lawrence Avenue to the beach. We make small talk and Todd notices I am different.

"What's up, Mike?" he asks.

I force a smile. "You're the third person today

who's asked me that. Nothing is wrong. It's July Fourth, Independence Day. We have to celebrate and become independent, don't we?"

Todd gives me a strange look and shrugs his shoulders. "Yeah, I guess so."

We stop and buy a soda from Whitey. He's been the soda man on the beach for years. He's almost as much a part of the summer as the tourists. Most of the people on the beach are strangers. The townspeople usually stay at home.

We do our beach routine, stripping down to our suits and spreading out the blanket. Todd surveys the beach for the prettiest girls and we sit near them. I know he loves Dee, but I guess he figures there's no harm in looking.

Todd gets out the Coppertone and coats his body. I've always hated greasy lotions but Todd says they give you a better tan. Perhaps he's right because he looks like a bronzed young god, while I look like a brown Indian. In the street behind the beach, kids are throwing firecrackers.

"They should wait until dark," Todd says.

Dogs bark. The waves make a lapping noise. Somewhere a baby cries. Today I am acutely aware of life.

We sun ourselves, then we take a swim, then we throw the Frisbee around a little. It's a day like so many other days before it. At three, mothers start to pack their babies up and the beach crowd thins considerably. It's quieter after four. Most of the children have gone home—for dinner or for their naps.

"I'm starved," Todd says. "Let's have a hot dog." We race through the sand, which by now is very hot, and buy super hot dogs from Whitey.

We eat and we make small talk. "I got a card from Dee and she really misses me," he says. "She's having an awful time."

"It's hard being separated from someone you love," I say.

We finish our hot dogs and then we lie back and listen to the radio.

"How come Jeffie didn't want to come today?"

"He did but I told him it would be too crowded," I say.

"My sister wanted to come too," Todd says. "We should take them to the fireworks tonight."

The ones tonight or the ones that will take place when I tell you the truth? I've never done anything this hard in my life. I have so much I want to say to Todd and so little courage to say it with.

I worry about his reaction. But I have to tell him. I've been promising myself that I would for a long time.

Todd actually starts the conversation. "Is something bothering you, Mike?"

I sit up on one elbow. "You could say that, Todd."

"Well, tell me," he urges. "What are friends for if you can't share things with them?"

My stomach feels as if a herd of angry bulls is stampeding around inside.

The day is drawing to a close and I know I've procrastinated long enough. The sun is streaking the sky and the beach is almost deserted.

"Todd, can we walk?"

He nods, sensing that something is about to happen. He walks beside me in a silence that's rare for him.

The waves slap at our feet as we walk. Finally we sit on the rock jetty and put our feet in the water.

"Listen, Mike, talk to me."

Todd's face is a study. The sunset gives him a rosy glow, adding to his tan, and his blue eyes seem piercing. His sun-streaked hair falls carelessly onto his forehead. God—I love him so much. Every instinct in me cries out to pull him close and to tell him I love him. But I fight those urges and speak.

"You're right, we do have to talk," I begin, "but you may not like what I have to say."

"It can't be that bad, Mike." His face softens and his hand touches my arm. Where his hand rests it feels as if my skin is burning. My face feels like it's on fire. I want to run. I want to throw up. I want to cry. But instead I look at Todd with steady eyes. He looks back at me. Our eyes are locked. "Well, Mike, tell me." His voice is soft and reassuring. "Tell me what's eating you up."

As he stares at me, he zips up his sweatshirt. The day is growing cool. A wind comes from the ocean. It's Independence Day, I hear my mind urge. Tell him. Tell him. The waves crash against the rocks, the sky darkens, and I swallow the lump that threatens to choke me. I say it. "Todd—I'm gay."

The world does not end. God doesn't appear. Angels don't trumpet. The earth is still intact. The only sounds are the hungry gulls, the patient lapping of the waves and the pounding of my heart.

I search Todd's face for clues. A single tear makes its way down his face. When he speaks his voice is quiet. "So. That's what it is."

That's all. No damnation. No screaming. No anger. No running from me. Instead he pulls me close to him. "You've carried this secret around for more than a year, haven't you?"

I nod my head, for if I speak, I'm certain I will cry.

"I've known about that long," Todd says quietly, without any difference in his voice. "I think perhaps I've known even longer than that. That's why I took you to the Village. That's why I've encouraged you to talk about it. But before now, you haven't been ready. It's okay, Mike. Really it's okay. I'll help you through this in any way that I can."

He is still Todd of the teddy-bear and blood-brother days. My heart sings. He knew. He knew even before I knew and he never pulled away.

"I didn't tell you because I thought if you knew, you'd hate me."

"Hate you?" He sounds distressed. "Hate you? I love you, shithead. I've always loved you. Not romantically, of course, but in a deeper way. I could punch you for thinking that. Why did you carry it all alone? Whenever I need you, you're there. That means more to me than anything. We are part of each other. Because you're gay and I'm straight doesn't alter that. You're Mike. The same Mike I've fought with and loved for so many years. I hate the thought that you were afraid to tell me. What finally made you decide to tell me?"

"It was either that or go crazy."

Todd and I are both crying by now. We wipe our eyes with our hands but the tears don't stop. They are not tears of sorrow, but tears of joy, happiness, relief.

"Do your parents know?" I say they don't. "I'll help you tell them," he offers.

I'll be glad for his support when the time comes.

Long after the sun goes down, Todd and I sit on the rock jetty and talk. It's Independence Day and I have been set free.

EPILOGUE

A YEAR and a half has passed since the day I told Todd. Once he knew, things just sort of fell into place. The world righted itself in my mind and I could go on.

Shortly after I told Todd, I told Dad. He was understanding and he cautioned me about letting the gay stuff become overpowering and ruining my life. He also said he loved me the same, gay or straight, and that means more to me than anything else he could have said. He told Mom. She was more upset and cried for a while, but then, as is typical of her, she started to read and educate herself on the subject.

I'd like to say that Steve reacted favorably, but he didn't. He roared and yelled and wanted to put me through a wall. In fact, he hardly speaks to me and our relationship is strained. We have a sort of truce. I don't mention it and neither does he. One night he did say he was trying to resolve the whole issue, and he told me he still loves me. I guess that's all I can expect from him.

Of course, Jeffie is unaware of anything yet. He's growing every day and since I'm away at college, he's taken to writing me letters. His letters are the hit of the dorm. Somehow, I think when Jeff does find out, he'll accept it. He's more open and loving than Steve—less judgmental. He's more able to roll with the punches.

Trisha and Roger are engaged now and they drove up here to see me a few times. Telling her was hard, but once again I was surprised.

"No one can change what's inside of you, Mike," she said, her eyes a little misty. "I'm only sorry I couldn't have been what you needed." She kissed my cheek. "After all, you were my first love."

Todd remained supportive in a way that is unbelievable. He encouraged me to get involved in the gay movement, and even went to meetings with me. He and Dee are talking about getting married, and of course I'll be the best man.

It's taken a long time for me to sort out my feelings about Todd, but now I have peace within myself where he's concerned. I can never expect more from him than what I already have. He is my best friend. Our souls are meshed in a bond that can never be severed by anything. He can never be my lover. I have dated several guys here at college but as of yet there is no one special. I hope someday there will be.

I still treasure my fantasies about Todd, but his friendship is real and that's what's really important.

Another good thing happened. Foxie's son came home. It was a time of celebration and it made Foxie the happiest man alive. Gary thanked me for being there when his dad needed someone.

I'm taking the courses I need to become a counselor to gay kids who are going through what I went through. If I could say one thing to people about the subject of homosexuality it would be to ask them to open their minds a little bit. None of us has chosen this. It has chosen us. We are the same people as you are. We feel, we love, we need to be accepted. Don't shut us out. All we want to do is to lead full lives and be happy—that's all anyone wants.

B. A. ECKER grew up in Somerville, New Jersey. She attended Rutgers University and then worked as a reporter for eight years on *The Ocean County Reporter* in Toms River, New Jersey. Ms. Ecker, who is also a photographer, currently lives in Venice, California, where she is working on her next novel.